LUCKY TRIGGER

THE SALVATORE BROTHERS SERIES BOOK 1

V. ELIAS

First published by Self Published 2026

Cover art by V. Elias
Email: v.eliasauthor@gmail.com

ISBN-13: 979-8-9947331-3-4

AUTHOR NOTE

Lucky Trigger is a dark, stand-alone mafia romance. It is the first book of the Salvatore brothers series. It does contain content and situations that could be triggering to some readers. This book is explicit and has explicit sexual content, intended for readers 18+.

I am listing the list of triggers, please read them before you actually read the book or read at your own risk. Happy readings.

Content Warning & Tropes:

- Mature content
- Kidnapping/ Human Trafficking
- Drug/Weapon mentions
- Surprise Pregnancy
- Sexual Abuse
- Death
- Age-Gap
- Mafia/ Organized Crime
- Cheating

- Forbidden/ Taboo
- Forced Proximity
- Bad Boy/ Good Girl
- Billionaire
- He Falls First

ACKNOWLEDGMENT

I would like to acknowledge my family for supporting all the way through this process. When I decided to right my own book, I was a bit hesitant because I didn't know what the process would be like. I had to learn everything on my own. I became a self published author in 2026 but I started writing and brainstorming about my books for a long time. I always loved English and Literature subjects in high school. I always wanted to write my own books but always stopped myself because of my insecurities. Then in 2025, my husband gifted me a kindle which pushed me to read lots of books. I became so in love with all the stories that I came across that I wanted to tell the world to read them too. I started reviewing books for fun and making videos about it on TikTok. My first reviews weren't watched by many but it was okay because I was starting barely. Then one day I posted a book review about a book that was dark romance, that got many likes, views and comments. The video ended up having 179.8k views, 1,417 likes, 73 comments, 1,144 saves and 73 people reposted the video. To this day this is my most viewed video. This gave me the inspiration to keep going with the reviews. The booktok community is so passionate and since I had a certain algorithm in my feeds. I came across a video where the person talks about how to be self published. I started researching and dedicated my time to learning all I could. I got a message from a new book author wanting for me to review her book, she also inspired me to do what I love. Now every time I see a new book author sharing a post about their book, I engage with their video. I will always be thankful to those people and my family because they never stopped believing in me.

The making of these books have been so fun and a great experience. I always were obsessed with Italian Mafia and Age-gap book, so I decided to make one of my own. The story is straight out of my imagination. I spent hours, days, months brainstorming and writing. The editing and formatting process wasn't easy but what in life is easy? Nothing really. I need to be thankful to my older sister for being my beta reader and my editing partner. She has been my go to girl for all of my books. My husband as well, he was my beta reader and of course his suggestions were taken into consideration even though you know some men don't know about romance books. I just want to appreciate and be thankful for the people that takes the time to review, read and share their feedback with me because that's what makes me grow and be better for next time.

Thank you to all the readers, I write books to share my passion for romance. I want readers to get into the scene to picture the characters in their mind while reading. I want readers to be able to relate to the story or to even imagine it so they get that little sensation you get in your heart or tummy when you read a romance scene. All I ever wanted to do was to be able to share my imagination and share the romance I create in my head. Thank you again for trusting me with your happy readings. I hope you enjoy the 3 book series of these 3 Italian brothers. You will want to read all of them.

CHAPTER 1

LUCIANO "LUCKY"

Every year is the same, I've been dealing with this shit for I don't know how many years. I have been in charge of everyone's mess. I have to fix everything when it comes to the job. My father made me in charge of the Cosa Nostra Organization at the short age of eighteen. Why? Because he said that I was a man already and that I needed to take over so he could step down. All I wanted was a normal life but I was forced into this. Giuseppe Salvatore, my father, was my biggest fear and enemy but he was also my biggest inspiration. My father made me look up to him. I always wanted to be like him when I grew up but that all changed when I was forced into the organization and saw all the horrible things that came with the job. I was in disbelief the first day I was put on the job. My father made me watch every gruesome action his puppets did to a poor ma, who was on the ground half beaten to death. All I remember was the splattered blood in every corner of that tiny room. That day will always be engraved in my brain. I stared at his empty eyes, no remorse from my father, the man that was supposed to show my brothers and I to be good people shuddered everything with his actions. My father's puppets ended the poor man's life right in front of my eyes. I didn't know the reason for my father's doing until I asked him once we left the warehouse, he said that this happens to anyone that dares to betray and disobey his orders. The man in front of my eyes was my father's worker, who had one job assigned which was to kill someone and he failed to do so. The man did not complete the task which enraged my father then later decided to make an example out of him. At eighteen, I learned the ins and outs of the job. I was never permitted to go study a career because my father said I wasn't going to learn anything good from that, instead he taught me how to use a gun. The first gun I ever held in my hand was a pistol; a Beretta 92. I learned how to dismantle, load and unload that baby. My father hired a personal boxer to train me. I didn't even know why it would be needed but he said it was necessary for the job. When he started trusting me with more important things, he let me take charge of the accounting side of the drug business. My father knew I was good with numbers, he made me do audits for all the money that came in and out. After working with numbers, he said I was ready for the next step which I thought it was fast. He said he would ease me into the hard parts of the job so he thought working with numbers first would be easier but what came next was something shocking to me, it repulsed me. He called me one night after finishing the audits to tell me that he needed me at the warehouse. When I got there, my father guided me into the tiny room, the same room I once saw that man's life get taken away. When I stepped inside I saw another man that was tied up in a chair. He told me that he had betrayed us. At that moment I was confused as to why I was needed but then I put two and two together, he needed me to finish the job. He extended a pistol for me to take, telling me to show him that I could really take over the family business, to be the man he needed me to be. I've never wanted to disappoint my father but in the position I'm in at the moment I hated everything about him, I don't want to kill but I'm being forced to. I did not take the pistol from his hands at first, I froze. I couldn't do what he was asking me to do. Giuseppe then yelled at me,

"Ascolta, figlio mio, o togli di mezzo quell'uomo con questa pistola, o te ne pentirai amaramente."[1] * (Listen, my son, either get rid of that man with this gun, or you will regret it bitterly.)

That was the first time I've ever seen my father be so curt with me. I took the gun from his hands, shaking as if the room was below zero but it was just me, I'm holding the gun with my two hands, aiming straight towards the man that equally stared back at me with remorse. I can feel the sweat dripping down my forehead as I'm looking for an escape. My father yells at me again but this time, when I look at him his chin dipped once giving me a single nod knowing that I was about to make a life changing decision. I squeezed the trigger feeling the recoil kicking back with force. All I can think of "It's done, I did it, my dad it's going to be proud" but all I'm feeling is regret. I see the dead man in front of me, blood oozing from the bullet hole. I step out of the tiny room clutching my stomach "I'm going to be sick", you know that sour taste you get in your mouth when you know you are about to empty your stomach by throwing up everything you ate that morning, yeah that's me at this very moment. Behind me, my father tapped my shoulder "Son, you did great. We will take care of the rest, go home." I jumped into my bike and drove for hours until I was able to calm myself down somehow. My face felt the breeze of the wind pass by while I drove and drove without stopping or no destination in mind. I went home but couldn't stop thinking of the man I murdered. I wanted to go to the only person that could've console me; my mother Theresa Salvatore. My mother was my angel, she had always shown her empathy for people. She helped a lot of them with her kindness, love and from time to time volunteered to help her community. My mother was the one who taught us English since she was born in New York. While we all lived in Italy most of the time, we traveled to New York when our father had business to attend to. It makes me sick to my stomach

1. Listen, my son, either get rid of that man with this gun, or you will regret it bitterly.

that people hurt her. My mother died at the hands of bad people, people like us. She was found murdered, I remember it as if it was yesterday. I had turned sixteen, I was coming out of our house when a black van pulled up next to the entrance and dumped her right in front of my eyes. I will never forget that man's evil smirk when he tossed my mother's lifeless body in front of me. No one knows why they did it. My father told me he searched for the people who murdered her but didn't find anything. My brothers and I were devastated to have lost the only person that made us believe that we could do good in this world. I promised myself that I would find whoever was responsible for the death of my mother and when I find them, I will end their life the same way they ended hers. I didn't have anyone else that could take me in their arms to tell me that everything was going to be alright. I decided to go to the bar to drown my sorrows. The bar was full of people at this hour, which bothered me, I didn't want to talk to anyone. Without any more thoughts in mind, I sat my ass down on a stool facing the bartender.

"Datemi un Negroni e continuate a portarmene altri."[2] * (Give me a Negroni and keep them coming.)

The bartender poured my drink on the rocks. Even though I was eighteen at the time, everyone knew me and they never dared to refuse alcohol to a mafia boss. I was known as the youngest mob boss and most people do what I want when I throw a little bit of money their way. While drinking, a red-haired girl introduced herself as Serafina, leaning on my shoulder she asked me if I was looking for a good time. The first time I've ever been with a girl was when my father paid a prostitute to have sex with me. I didn't want to but he told me that I needed to be a man. I've had my fair share with women and most are willing to kiss my feet and while I was here to forget that I just killed a man, I still followed her. My mind kept telling me that she might be able to relieve some tension, and maybe let me forget what happened tonight. I took her to the back of

2. Give me a Negroni and keep them coming.

the bar by the bathroom stalls where it was dark, I cornered her pushing her on her knees and I made her suck my cock. She took me pretty deep and with teary eyes she took my cock to the back of her throat, gagging and then composing herself to do it all over again. After emptying my cum in her mouth, I took the condom that was in my wallet and slid it on my cock. I lifted her from the kneeling position she was in, she was light as a feather. Positioning myself at the entrance of her glistening pussy, I pushed my cock inside her making her moan. I covered her mouth with one hand to stop her from making it known to people that I was fucking her. I thrusted hard pushing my cock in and out of her multiple times until I could feel her squeezing it with her pussy. I emptied my cum inside the condom as she came with me. I softly put her back on her feet, grabbing my wallet from my pants, I took out 100 euros to give to her. When I handed the money to her, she looked at me in disbelief. I didn't see it coming but she struck me across the face telling me that she didn't want my money and that she wasn't a prostitute. I was in shock at the strike, I shouldn't have assumed she was a prostitute. After the misunderstanding, I apologized heading towards the exit. I was in no condition to drive my bike, I had to sober down before I could head home. I went back inside to get a couple of water bottles, sitting outside on the curb drinking water and waiting to get sober, I took out my phone to dial my brother. It was after one in the morning, my brother Joey known as "Ace" was always awake at this time. My brother would be either watching TV or playing video games.When I dialed the house phone it rang three times, but he did not pick up so I took it as a sign that something was wrong. I called one of my dad's guys to come pick me up since I still wasn't able to drive my bike. When I got there I pushed the double doors of our mansion, the place I call home. Everything was quiet on the first floor and dark except as I kept walking, I could hear the wailing cry of one of my brothers. I ran past the stairs to get to Ace's room but there was no sign of him there. I ran to Alessandro's room finding Joey hugging Alessandro so hard he could crack his bones.

"Ace, what happened?" There were no words, just an uncontrollable cry. I shook him a little to get him to respond.

"Lucky, dad beat Alessandro so hard, I couldn't help him. I wanted to, I really did but I was afraid, you gotta believe me" I could hear his frantic voice.

"Ace, I believe you, you couldn't have done anything, you are barely thirteen years old. Now tell me the reason why our father hit Alessandro?"

I was seeing red because once Ace left his tight hold on Alessandro, he turned to me to show me the aftermath of the beating. Alessandro's legs and arms were quickly bruised.

"Lucky, dad found out that Alessandro broke something important to him but it was an accident I swear. Dad called Alessandro "chaos" because he said mom didn't raise him like you and I! He said that she baby him too much"

The rage that was going through my veins was making my blood boil. I couldn't stand up to my father, he was the same man who just made me kill a man tonight. I told myself that this would be the last time I let anyone put their hands on my brothers. I treated Alessandro's wounds but the more I cleaned them up, I could see my little brother shed more tears, I couldn't stand it anymore. I got up and told Ace to stay with him, to not move for any reason even if he heard our father's yelling. My steps were heavy, not thinking of what I was going to say to my father once we were face to face. I went by his room, he wasn't there so I stepped inside his office where he was sitting down already with a reeking smell of alcohol. I slammed the door, making him turn my way.

"Son, to what do— do I owe the— the pleasure" I was furious, there is no way in hell he was this relaxed, his slurred words lets me know that he is drunk. I charged in his direction slamming my fist on his desk,

"Why the fuck did you hit my brother, he is five years old!"

My father stood up rounding his desk, took a slight step in front of me and smacked me in the face. I took it like a man but I also didn't back down, I took advantage that he wasn't sober and pushed him off me.

"The next time you decide to hit any of my brothers you will answer to me". With my father laying on the floor he raised his hand to shoo me away. At least that was the last time he physically put his hands on my brothers."

I CAN'T BELIEVE that happened so long ago. It's been fifteen years since that encounter. My father has officially stepped down from the business passing everything over to me. I have taken over mostly everything, while I took charge of the drug operation, the gun distributions, and money laundering. Ace was in charge of our nightclub and brothel when he turned twenty-one. My father put him in charge of that because he knew Ace was the life of the party, he gets along with everyone, he knows how to work with the ladies we employ. He doesn't mix business and pleasure but he does meet a few girls here and there at the nightclub where he ends up taking them back to a hotel. He has never been the one to settle down or want kids, he is just having too much fun to think about that. We all still live in the mansion but we also have our own penthouses to make it easier on us when we want to bring girls around. I am too busy to be with women but I pay for sex from time to time. While Ace manages that side of the job, I told Alessandro not to worry about getting involved in this. I wanted my little brother to live a normal life while Ace and I deal with this shit. At least I can't complain, he is a kind person, going to school and getting a career just how we wanted him to. I wanted him to have everything we didn't. He chose the most popular school in Sicily, Italy. The university of Palermo is known as the best school in Sicily. Alessandro got named "Chaos" by our father when he was little and the nickname just got stuck with him throughout the years. Our father wanted to help raise Alessandro but I took over that, knowing that he did not have any patience with him. The only thing I couldn't stop was that our father wanted Alessandro to have an arranged marriage with his friend's daughter in order to get more connections for our business. I tried to stop him but failed miserably, however I told him to let Alessandro turn twenty one to let the marriage happen. He agreed, but now it's just a ticking bomb waiting for him to turn twenty one in a few months.

CHAPTER 2

OLIVIA

Blowing my twenty candles and putting a fake smile on my face for all the people my gold digging mother invited. Yes! My mother! She never really cared for me or my dad, she only cared about his money. She stayed with him because she loved the financial stability my dad was able to provide for us. She was always cruel to him, even worse when it came to her only daughter, me! Hauling my mom to the kitchen so no one else can hear what I'm about to say.

"Mom, why did you invite all these people? You knew that I didn't want to celebrate my birthday."

She knows how difficult it is to celebrate my birthdays, I lost my father to cancer just days away from my birthday. Any time my birthday comes, all I want is to surround myself with him even if it's at the cemetery without people prying. My birthdays used to be special when my dad was around. He always had something planned that made me get out of the house and have a day full of fun things. My father was the most loving, caring father. He basically raised me on his own while still working to provide for us. My mother always said that she was not fit to be a mother but she still wanted to stay without having to be responsible for me. My father told me to understand her, because she was a young mother. Her other excuse was that she had gone through postpartum depression, but she never sought medical help. It's been exactly two years since my dad's passing and it isn't getting any better, the ache in my heart is still there even after two years of him being gone.

"Gosh Liv, I tried doing something good and you treat me this way? I can't ever understand you!"

"Mom, my name is not Liv, it's Olivia! Please don't call me that"

She knew exactly which buttons to push to get a reaction out of me. She knows that I hate when anyone calls me Liv. I was just waiting for this shit show to be over so I can hide in my room for the rest of the night. Moving the cake from the kitchen island, I pushed it to the back of the refrigerator. Came out of the kitchen to mingle with the people my mother invited, I didn't even know half of them. As I was talking to one of my mom's friends. My best friend walked through the main door. Thank God, she always knows when to show up and it's always when I need her the most.

"Excuse me, I need to go say hi to my best friend" My mom's friend patted me on the back as I stood up from the couch to make my way towards my best friend.

"Anna, omg! Thank you for coming, for saving me from all these people I barely know"

"Happy birthday bestie, don't thank me! I always know when you need me so here I am. So what should we do" We needed to make a plan on how to ditch this party "my own party". Anna knows I'm not into partying or drinking, but she wants me to have fun for once since I haven't had fun since the day of my father's passing.

"Olivia, let's go out partying, It's your birthday. You only turn twenty years old once. Come on! Let's go"

"No, I don't want that. I just want to relax in my room, maybe read a book or sketch a new design for my portfolio"

"No! That is boring! We need to have fun on your special day. Let's call Christian so he can take us somewhere"

"Unfortunately, Christian told me he was going to be at practice and wasn't going to make it to my birthday."

Christian is my Quarterback boyfriend that I met at the beginning of college. We have been together for two years. He not only has shown up for me during my difficult times with the death of my father, but he is liked by everyone in my family, especially my mother. You can probably guess why my mother loves Christian so much. Yes... you guessed right, Christian is sitting on a golden pedestal. He has the contract of his life with his football team and his parents are wealthy. I never really cared for someone's social or financial status. I care deeply that the person I choose to be around provides me the same affection I provide them.

"Well that sucks! I can't believe Christian would prefer to go to practice than to be here with his girlfriend on her birthday."

Anna likes to exaggerate and always wants to make a big deal out of everything. I don't like that about her but I cannot change her ways because even though she is this way, I love Anna Collins. She is my best friend, we've known each other since high school, we share many things together, I don't want us to fight over this dumb shit.

"Anna, why don't you come with me to his practice maybe I can surprise him since he can't be here for me"

Anna drove her pretty BMW car that her father bought for her on her eighteenth birthday to the football field. We were about fifteen minutes away, since we all went to the same college, It was easy to get there. Our school was humongous, It was the best school in all of New York. We chose this school because we both wanted to be close to each other since we also go into the same fashion design program. I remember the day I met Christian Knowles, he was the most good looking guy from the rest of the guys on his team. Christian became the team captain for the New York Knights the first semester of college because of his impressive skills on the field. He is six foot tall with impressive abs that made me drool the first time I saw them. The first day I met Christian was the most embarrassing day for me. I was running late to school after spending all night in the hospital with my father. My energy was running low so I needed caffeine, heading to the coffee shop around the corner from the school I grabbed a cup of their double shot espresso to wake me up. I looked at the time on my watch and I was certain I was about to be late if I didn't run to class. I paid for my coffee and started running my way to school. Passing by the field to get to class, I should've tied my hair because it was all in my face blinding me, then suddenly I crashed into a hard wall. Not just any hard wall, It was the hard chest of the Quarterback on the football team. Without looking up I noticed that I had spilled the coffee on me. His blue eyes were set on mine offering his hand so I could stand up. I apologized telling him that I was an idiot, that it was all my fault I wasn't really paying attention or looking where I was going. He said it was okay, grabbing me by my wrists to help me up on my feet. When I stood there gazing at him, I couldn't believe I was talking to him so I froze in the moment. Then he took his fingers near my face to caress my cheek, snapping me awake, he said I had coffee on my cheeks. As soon as I looked down to see the mess I've made, I turned pink because my whole outfit was ruined. I couldn't go to class like that, then I remembered I needed to be in class but I was already late. After that embarrassing moment Christian started scoping me out any time I would walk by the field. He started to walk me to my car any chance he got until he made a move to ask me out on a date. I agreed to it, not because he was the sexiest guy I've ever met but because he took his time with me. Christian was my first! Everyone at school had already given up their virginity while I was still holding onto it for the right person which in this case was Christian. Since that day he has been the most perfect boyfriend I could've asked for. He came to my rescue so many times when I needed space from my mom, he spent time with me whenever I would leave the hospital devastated from seeing my father sick. I will never forget those moments because he was there for me.

"Look Anna, he is right there, number eleven. He looks so good in those tight pants huh?"

Anna made a face then ignored me. She didn't really like football players because she had a bad experience with one of them freshman year of college. From there she didn't really care for them and with Christian wasn't any different, she kept her distance any time he would be around me. She was cordial with him, she could talk to him to a certain point but then she will try to not over extend her friendliness to him. Once Christian saw me on the bleachers he paused the game telling his team to take a break. Everyone booed him at the moment he trotted towards me. I jumped from the bleachers to his hold while he spun me in circles, peppering me with kisses.

"Hi baby, what are you doing here? I thought your mom had a birthday party for you? Why aren't you there?"

"Nah, I didn't want to be there. But you know where I wanted to be? Here with you—"

He didn't even let me finish the sentence because he kissed me taking my breath away. When we pulled apart to look at each other he said he still had about thirty minutes more of practice. Once Christian had gone to the locker room to shower and get changed, we waited for him by the entrance of the parking area.

"Christian is taking forever, why don't you go check if he is almost ready"

Anna was being impatient, I quickly turned back to the doors leading to the locker room where I found Christian talking to a girl very closely. I didn't like it, matter of fact I got jealous. He has never given me reasons to doubt him but seeing him this close to another girl just infuriated me. As I got closer and closer he saw me so he stepped back a few inches from the girl while her hand came up to caress his cheeks and he stopped her. I stood in front of the girl introducing myself as his girlfriend, her eyes widened at the declaration. She gave me a smile before turning to get out of there. I turned to face my boyfriend, he practically shrugged because he did not want to have a confrontation. Instead of harassing him with questions I decided to let it go. I don't want to ruin a relationship that has been good for the past two years.

"Should we go now? I was thinking about going back home and hiding in my room. Maybe you and Anna can be there for support, you guys can drink if you like"

He knows that I don't really like drinking like that, I just have bad memories growing up when mom used to drink a lot. I kind of promised myself to never repeat her behavior with alcohol. I could drink for special events but not on a regular basis.

"Yeah, let's go, I have a surprise for you in the car"

Christian is smirking so hard which makes me think he did something I told him not to do. I have told him and Anna that they do not need to give me anything for my birthday. Anna of course listened to my request but Christian wasn't one of them. There is no doubt he didn't care about my request; he still got me a gift. Anna drove her car back to my house while I became the passenger princess in Christian's car. Once home, we got in through the side door just in case there were still people celebrating "my birthday", a birthday that I didn't even want. We ran up to my room and immediately locked it, my mom didn't need to be in this room. That night was one of the best nights I've had in a really long time. Christian gave me the gift he bought for me, he had bought a new portfolio since the one I have is already almost filled. A very thoughtful present, he knows that my dream is to get into the study abroad program which will be in Italy for six months to get my degree. I signed up for the program but I was late signing in. They had told me that I was on the waiting list. They didn't give me an estimated time, now I have to wait for some miracle like maybe a student dropping out or magically a spot will open up giving me access to being next in line.

CHAPTER 3

LUCIANO 'LUCKY"

"Boss, we have a shipment coming in today at three. Should we distribute it or keep it in the warehouse?"

The shipment contains just about everything from narcotics, ammunition, and weapons. Our biggest distributors are from South America. Colombia and Peru to be exact. This is the reason I had to learn a little bit of Spanish in order to communicate with the people I do business with.

"Matteo, stop calling me boss, you know you can call me "Lucky". We have been best friends for years. There is no need to be professional when it's just us."

I met Matteo when he turned eighteen. His parents are really good friends with my father, they used to make him come to the house so I could get to know him. When we met I didn't really like him, one because he was way too young to be my friend even though I was only twenty one when we met and two because we had nothing in common. After we kept talking we started to kind of like the same things, we bonded over music. We both love to listen to classical music, which is odd for a young person to listen to. Matteo always tells me that we have an old soul. I always liked how people used to do things back then, like write letters, dedicate songs, no electronics, and how people could bond over a meal at the dinner table. Nowadays, no one sits down on the dinner table, they eat on the go. Most are stuck on their phones, instead of calling, people text all the time.

"Fine! Lucky we need to know what we need to do with this shipment. They need word fast to have everything settled once they get here"

Matteo has been my right hand man from the day he showed me I could trust him. I'll never forget the day he saved my life. That day was a regular business day, but somehow something went wrong and I was needed at the port. That day my father had invited Matteo's parents for drinks, they had come to the house with him. When I told dad that I needed to go resolve a little issue at the port he suggested I take Matteo with me. I hesitated to take him with me because he was still young, I didn't want to involve him in our world. Father insisted I take him with me, leaving me no other choice. I told him to wait for me in the car. I went to the office to grab my pistol, clipping it inside my leather jacket. I quickly left towards my Cadillac that was parked in front of the house. When I got inside he had a big ass smile that I wanted to slap away. He does not know what he just got himself into. I should've declined my father's suggestion to bring him with me. I got to the port, getting out of the car to meet our contact. I paused for a second, turning my face to speak to Matteo. I told him to stay in the car, I also warned him that there was another pistol inside the car just in case something happens to me. I left the keys inside to give Matteo a chance to escape just in case everything went to shit. I headed to the contact, not even a minute had passed when the shooting started. They had followed my contact to the port, putting all of us in danger. My gaze kept going back and forth from the people shooting to where Matteo was in my car. I pulled my pistol from the inside of my jacket, shooting into the direction of the people shooting back at us. I checked my other clipped side of my jacket to get the second magazine I had but I wasn't finding it, it must have fallen out in the process of me running to cover myself from the gun shots. Everything happened so quick, I looked down for just a second, then when I returned my gaze back up to where the people were shooting, I found a man staring back at me with a pointed gun on my forehead. He almost had that same evil smirk on the guy that dropped my mother's body in front of me. I saw my life flash before me, knowing that it would be my last day on earth. I closed my eyes waiting for the hit or the gunshot wound. It never came, I opened my eyes to see the man laying on the floor knocked out, Matteo had gotten out of the car to save my life. He used the bottom of the gun to knock him unconscious. He really did save me from getting killed. That was the day I knew that he would be down for anything. He became my best friend, a brother and my right hand man. I have him in charge of the small stuff that doesn't need my attention. He has been able to handle most of it without needing me since I'm always busy with other crap that I have to deal with on a daily basis but he has been a good friend, he always has my back.

"Tell the guys to get the warehouse ready, to have all imports go through the warehouse and then from there we can distribute it to the paying organizations. Oh, before I forget, in today's shipment we are getting an extra import for the Camorra clan, they are paying a little bit extra to have it delivered. I can't deliver it myself but I'm going to send "Chaos" to hand deliver it since he is good friends with Luca Rossi."

"You got it Lucky, I'll meet you later to go over the numbers of the shipment"

I head out to meet with the 'Ndrangheta organization because they want to talk about their cocaine importation so we have to talk business and money a lot more money. The Camorra and the 'Ndrangheta are the main organizations we do a lot of business with. We do business with a lot more but those have to be our main ones since they bring more money in. Then that money goes through our nightclub, brothel and many other businesses we have to launder it. At times I don't want to be involved in any of this but since my father appointed me as the head of the operations, I got to deal with mostly everything. I have no life. I think it is also the reason why I haven't settled down with a woman or want kids, this is no life for them. It's one of the reasons why I want Alessandro to stay away from all of this since Joey is already involved and can't really pull him out. He loves this shit. He was born to lead. It scares me to see him so invested in the job he is in charge of, he is also good with numbers and deals with everything from the nightclub and the brothel so I don't have to.

"Good afternoon gentleman, are we ready to talk business?"

Everyone sitting on the table nodded their heads. They want to collaborate with their cocaine imports with us, we need a set amount on how much money we are putting in.

"Our contacts for our imports are mainly from South America, our guy is coming from Peru. He is bringing the good stuff, how about we do 60% for us and 40% for you? That way we are getting some profit"

"How about we do 50% each and I can pitch either weapons or protection from our organization?"

"Let me talk to the big boss and I'll call you later with an answer"

I shake everyone's hands then I head out to go back home to talk to Chaos. He is home right now finishing some work for school. Opening the double doors from our mansion I hear my father yelling in his office. I quickly step inside to see what's going on, finding Alessandro sitting down across my father's chair. Giuseppe is yelling at the top of his lungs telling Alessandro that he needs to go out on a date with the girl he has been set for the arranged marriage. Chaos is telling him that he does not want to, that he is not in love with this girl. He looks to me for some kind of help but I cannot give it to him because I made dad promise to not put his hands on him, to wait for him to turn 21 to set him up with the arranged marriage so I shrug my shoulders letting him know I can't do shit. Trying to de-escalate the tension in the room I got in the middle of both of them, turning my attention to Chaos I tell him to let me talk to dad.

“Why can’t we forget about this arrangement? Did you already sign a contract or something with the Esposito family?”

“No..not yet, but this needs to happen Luciano! We need this contact so we can expand our family business.”

“No, we don’t dad, I got this under control. We don’t have to bring anyone in to expand. I just met with the ‘Ndrangheta and we are going to expand on the cocaine portion!” I’m already getting exhausted from raising my voice, my father was taking no for an answer.

“No Luciano, the arrangement is done! Chaos will marry after his twenty-first birthday to Leila Esposito! This will happen even if you try to prevent it! Now, please get out of my office!” my father slammed his fist on his desk. I get out of the office speechless, I pass by Ace’s room and then head to my little brother’s room. I knock on his door, he opens it letting me come in. He sits down at the edge of his bed waiting for me to talk.

“Dad is not going to budge, he is set on marrying you with the Esposito girl. I’ve tried everything, even tried to get new connections with other organizations so he is not inclined to keep this absurd arrangement but he is not going to give in. He wants this done and I don’t know what else I can do to stop it. I’m sorry bro, there’s nothing else I can do.” I can see my brother’s blank stare, he doesn’t know what else to do either. I don’t want him to do something he might regret, he will need to stick to this plan and hope that he either falls over heels for this girl or they live a miserable life together.

“It’s okay Lucky, I will go through with this arrangement. I’ll keep looking for a way to either get it annulled or divorced after a year. By that time our connections should be more established then I can leave this situation.”

My brother, already feeling defeated, sighs and shrugs. I tap his back as a sign of understanding the situation. I step out of his room to head to mine, once inside I start getting naked because I need a shower. In the shower I start thinking of how long it’s been since I had sex with anyone. Shit it's been months, the last one I had to pay for it. I trail my hands to touch the deep V line of my waist, I keep going until I'm cupping my dick in my hand. All I can think of is the pleasure of holding my dick in my hands, I start stroking it once, twice until it becomes natural to keep stroking. Then I get the building up sensation of pleasure until I come on my hand releasing every tension I had. My balls tighten with the release making them sensitive. I clean up, then finish showering. I pick some shorts from my drawer with a plain black shirt and get inside the covers of my bed. The lack of sleep is already showing "under bags" in my eyes. I look at the time showing it's one in the morning, it must have passed like three hours from the time I fell asleep. Suddenly, my phone rings. Fuck, I can't ever get a good sleep because I am always needed.

"Hello—?"

"Lucky, it's Matteo sorry to call you at this time, I have been dreading this call but I don't think I can keep hiding this from you. I thought I could get ahead of this before you to fix it but it seems like it's bigger than what it seems. I don't think I could do this on my own, that's why I'm calling. I know you are probably going to be mad. I didn't tell you but I was trying to not cause you more work and stress on your end. Can we meet at the warehouse around six?"

Matteo's restrained voice could give me some clues of the seriousness of the conversation.

"Matteo— No! I am not waiting until six for you to tell me what the fuck is going on! We are meeting now! I don't care if I have to drag you out of your house, meet me now at the warehouse...No— meet me here at my house, we will have more privacy here since everyone is sleeping."

Matteo didn't take long, he came in within minutes of the call. I waited for him outside the double doors to ensure he didn't ring the bell waking everyone up. He drives inside the gate, parking his car next to mine. Matteo gets out of his car, I can already see he is worried. His gaze kept fleeting around without making contact, hands rubbing against his legs, and his shoulders were tense.

"So—" didn't even finish my question, he cut me off by pulling me inside the house.

"Lucky, we need to go somewhere private. The conversation we need to have cannot get out from these four walls. This matter is serious and dangerous." He is scaring me, I don't get scared easily but his words are letting me know the seriousness of what's about to be said.

"Talk! Everyone is asleep, you can talk comfortably."

"Lucky, we have a "mole" this will affect all operations."

CHAPTER 4

OLIVIA

After the birthday fiasco ended on a good note because of my best friend and boyfriend, Anna and I met at school to take the exam we had been practicing for a while. I started working on a new piece for my portfolio and this will either let me ace the test or I will fail having to re-take it.

"Anna, are you ready for the exam? I studied everything that had to do with the measurements and sizes, I also brought my portfolio just in case I needed to refer back to it." I could sense something odd about Anna this morning. "Are you okay? Anna— hello? Earth to Anna—?"

"Sorry, I have a lot on my plate right now. I wasn't paying attention. What were you asking?"

" If you studied for the exam? Do you want to talk about it? You know I'm here for you."

"Olivia please stop! Why do you always have to be so nice, naive and so positive about everything— sorry I need to go" She started to leave but I grabbed her by her arm to stop her but she still pulled out of my hold to go towards the parking lot area. I don't know what the fuck just happened, I don't know where that came from. I am not naive! I'm the least positive person, from all that I have gone through, I learned to always think of the worst case scenarios. I need to call her to see what's going on. I pulled my phone from my bag to call her, it rang multiple times with no answer. Every time it would send me to her voicemail. I left one, but also decided to send her a message just in case she doesn't hear the voicemail.

"Anna, please tell me what happened? Is there anything I did? Can you call me or text me so we can talk about it.?"

hitting send on the text message, it showed as delivered.

Christian suddenly grabs me by the waist from behind making me jump scare.

"Oh my god, you scared me. What are you doing here? Don't you have practice right now?"

"I do, in fifteen minutes I just wanted to kiss and hug my girlfriend. Don't you have class soon?"

"Yeah, I do. Hey, can I ask you something?"

"Yeah what's up?"

"On the day of my birthday, when you took Anna home; did she seem okay? Did she say anything to you?" Christian had taken Anna home because she was still not sober. I told her that I would drive her car to her but the next morning she had sent someone to pick up her car.

"Mm... No, nothing. I took her home and then I went home..." I could sense some uncertainty in his voice but I let it go.

"Okay, well I have to go to class now. I'll see you after class right? We are going to your place for a bit before we have to come back for our next class?"

"Mhm, I'll wait for you at the lockers okay."

I gave him a kiss goodbye, then quickened my step to the direction of my class. I took my exam, it was so much information that I feel like I missed some things. Anna was nowhere to be found, she didn't take the exam which it's 80% of your grade. That made me worry even more for her because she has never missed an exam before. I don't know why she does not want to tell me what's going on with her. I am her best friend, she should be able to talk to me, confide in me about her problems. After I finished my exam, I got out of the classroom and walked to the lockers. Finding Christian already dressed and showered we walked to his car. He drove us to his place, we had sex and then he took me back to school for my next class. As I was walking into campus I remembered I left my portfolio in Christian's kitchen table. My next class was starting in twenty minutes but I needed my portfolio for this class. I decided to risk it, so I went to my car and drove back to his place. Christian had given me a key to his place just in case I ever wanted to come relax between classes. I parked my car, walking to the stairs to his apartment. I pulled the keys from my bag. I opened the door, I didn't announce myself because as soon as I opened the door I saw a bag and girl shoes by the entrance.

I started to shake, I could feel my blood boiling, my fist was clenching at the situation in front of my eyes. I tiptoed towards Christian's room pausing when I heard a girl moaning.

"Oh, yes harder Christian—"

"You like this big dick inside your pussy." The bed kept squeaking with every thrust.

"Yes, yes— You can't ever tell her we did this okay, I don't want to lose her. Christian— oh my god—"

That voice was familiar to me, who is this girl? I grabbed the door knob turning it to open slightly but when I took another step the floor creaked making heads turn my way. I was already half way inside the room, I opened it all the way announcing myself but what I saw was something I never expected. I saw "my boyfriend and my best friend" together in bed. He was fucking her from behind. We literally just had sex an hour ago and he was now having sex but with my best friend! I couldn't stand the sight of them, I was seeing red. I couldn't believe what I was seeing, they were frozen in the moment, no words. I could see Anna's eyes tearing but was still in place. Christian moved first to cover himself, then threw Anna's clothes to her. I backed away from the room, grabbing my bag, my portfolio and my shoes. I took out the key Christian had given me to his place out of my key chain and left it on the kitchen table. I go to open the door but Christian positions himself between the door and myself to block me from leaving. With a sharp tone I told Christian to get out of my way but he wouldn't move. My mind kept going back to the picture of them in the same bed I was an hour ago. A knot in my stomach made me nauseous, I wish they would disappear from my sight, from my mind.

"Christian, move the hell away. Let me leave. We are done! Do not touch me!"

"Olivia baby, please don't— please it doesn't mean anything, I swear."

"I don't care, we are done and you— (pointing at Anna) we are also done! Best friends don't do this to each other. Anna! you can have him, I don't want him!"

"Olivia, I'm sorry— please forgive me. I never meant for this to happen. It just happened recently. I made a mistake—"

I struck her across the face, not caring anything in the world about the consequences. They tore me up with their actions, I was numbed at this point. No rage, no blood boiling. All I wanted was to be out of there. I pushed Christian out of the way, running down the stairs I got to my car and drove away. I was already ten minutes late to class but I didn't care I needed the distraction. Sitting down near the front to pay attention to the professor, I took out my portfolio and got to perfecting my design. I didn't even take into account the minutes or the hour that had passed while finishing my design. The bell rang letting everyone know that the class had ended. I put my things inside my bag, and I start to make my way to the exit of the classroom. Then I got stopped by the professor,

"Olivia, do you have a minute to discuss something?"

"Yeah, is everything okay? Am I failing the class? Did I make a mistake on the homework?" Oh no, he was making a confused face, I can't read his facial expressions. Is he going to tell me bad news?

"No, no none of that Olivia, I just wanted to talk to you because I saw that you were listed on the waiting list for the study abroad program we have in school. Were you still interested in doing that?"

"Yes, I am. I signed up late in the semester and everything was occupied, but the lady that had the list outside the classroom told me to still sign up just in case a spot becomes available."

"Olivia, if you are serious about taking fashion designing abroad, I'll make it happen! I see so much potential in you, your drawings are getting better and better with practice. Your portfolio looks amazing, you are getting mostly A's in this class. If you want to get into the program a spot just opened up making you next on the list. The dean wanted to give it to another person since their parents are making a big donation but if you are serious about this, I'll make sure to advocate for you against the dean so you can go."

This is my opportunity, I want to go not only to get better at my drawings but to make this a career because I love fashion designing. I also want to leave to forget any of the shit that just happened. I want to be able to put some distance between my now ex-boyfriend and the traitor of a best friend I had.

"Yes professor, I am serious about this opportunity. I want to go study abroad, be able to learn a new language and get better at fashion design. Please let me be next in line."

"Okay Olivia, I will talk to the dean and your other fashion design professors to back me up. If you do end up going this is what's going to happen. First you will finish your portfolio with all of your designs here in class, second you will book your flight to Sicily, Italy. Third, you will stay in the dorms of the best university of Palermo. Fourth, you will work on getting better at the current drawings you already have with top tier professionals. Fifth, you will present them all at the tournament they will be having. Then lastly, you will come back home after six months of studying abroad to present your new portfolio to your professors here, then you will graduate with a degree in fashion design. How does that sound?"

Everything sounds so good, but I know it won't be that easy though. I have to plan this right. It's time for me to leave behind the things that don't bring me happiness. My mother has constantly been a reminder that I am not good enough for her. Now Christian has made me doubt myself. I don't understand what I did wrong, what was the reason for him cheating on me? I gave him everything I could've given him. Anna too! I was her best friend, why did she betray me this way? She didn't even like Christian to begin with. She always kept her distance, how is it that they got involved with each other? Was this the reason why she went off on me the other day?

"Professor Dean, I want everything you just mentioned to me. I want to be able to go abroad and study my passion. Fashion designing has been my dream since I was a little girl and used to dress up. I would always put my own touch to each outfit. When I started going to school, I got really good at designing. I want to do this, I know I can do it, please guide me how I can prove to the professors to let me get accepted into the program."

"Okay, we need to work really hard on how you will deliver your speech and how you will arrange your portfolio to match your speech. From there I'm sure they will have no other words than to say yes to your acceptance."

"Great, I can show you my portfolio now and I can work on my speech at home today and have it ready by tomorrow. I can draft it and then you can let me know if anything needs to be edited."

"That sounds great, I'll see you tomorrow after class"

I went home to get everything ready, I couldn't get unfocused but as I was putting my portfolio on my desk to get started my mom knocked on my door. She enters the room to let me know Christian is downstairs wanting to speak to me. I told her I didn't want to see him but she insisted that I should make the effort to talk to him. I didn't want to have to explain but she left me no other choice.

"Mom, I do not want to talk to Christian, you keep insisting that I talk to him but If you knew what he did then you wouldn't keep telling me to talk to him"

"Liv, what did he do? He has been the best boyfriend you ever had."

"Mom, stop calling me Liv, you know I hate that nickname! I don't want to see Christian, I found him cheating on me with my best friend Anna!"

"I knew it! I knew she was a little whore! I never really liked her. Liv! You need to take claim on your man, go talk to him and forgive him. Men make mistakes, your dad made many mistakes and I forgave him multiple times. Please just go and take him back."

Was she serious? Why would she even suggest that I should take him back? I have dignity and I am not going to forget he did this to me. Since my mom is not going to tell him to leave, I will! I walked past my mother and she follows right behind me. When I get to the living room, Christian is sitting down on the couch waiting for me. With my eyebrows drawn and a sharp tone I begin to yell at him.

"Christian! Please leave! I do not want to see you ever again!

"Liv, don't be rude!"

"Mom, stop!"

"Christian, we are over! What you did is unforgivable! You had sex with my best friend and just hours before that, you had sex with me! I don't even want to begin to imagine, if you've done this with other women while being with me. I need to get myself tested. You are such an asshole! Please leave! Never come back, forget that I exist!"

Pushing Christian towards the door, he kept on apologizing saying she didn't mean anything but I cannot forget their voices, their moaning and their faces when I caught them. Once I pushed him out the door, my mom drew her eyebrows together and told me that I was going to regret my decision. Turning away from her I head back to the room because I really need to get started on my speech and portfolio for tomorrow.

CHAPTER 5

OLIVIA

I got up super early to finalize everything on my speech with my designs. I got in my car then drove to school. Once there I went to class, my leg kept shaking because the clock on the wall was about to point to the time when class ended. Hearing the bell rang, sweat trickled down my spine at the thought of Professor Dean reading my speech. I spaced out for a bit before coming to my senses hearing him call my name.

"Olivia? Earth to Olivia, are you ready?

"Yes, sorry I spaced out. I'm really nervous"

"It's okay to be nervous, this is a big deal for you. Shall we get started?"

While he read my speech and looked at each design I had, he kept his eyes going back and forth between my speech and I. He hadn't given me any clue about my speech, the whole time he was quiet and kept making notes on my paper.

"Well Olivia, this is actually the best stuff you have ever written in my class. I wrote a few things to fix but other than that you are ready. You will present this tomorrow to all the professors, your portfolio is looking great."

"I'm super excited but I am also nervous to mess up my opportunity. Thank you again for helping me pull this through. I'm hoping to be ready for tomorrow"

" Don't hope Olivia, you have to be ready because this is a life changing experience. Be ready tomorrow at noon."

I went home, happiness bloomed inside me just thinking about tomorrow. If they accept me into this program, I will be leaving soon and I will have the space I need from everyone. I'll also get to experience something I love to do. Woke up feeling insecure, anxiety swirled throughout my body. I got up from my bed and ran to have a cold shower. Maybe this will ease some tension. By the time I was done and dressed, the rumbles in my stomach indicated that I was hungry. There was no way my mom would have breakfast ready for me so I decided to leave a little early to go through the nearest fast food drive thru to pick up some donuts. I got to school just in time to review and practice on my speech. The doors opened up letting me know I was next, professors were all seated, all eyes on me. I had printed a few paper sizes of my design to provide to each professor while I had my portfolio open for them to see as well. They introduced themselves first then asked for me to introduce myself. One of the male professors told me to begin my speech, my heart was in my throat by the time I finished talking. They all got up clapping and congratulating me on a well done presentation. They told me that I have to wait until tomorrow to see the list of who passed outside the classroom around noon. I went back to professor Dean's class to let him know that I have a good feeling about it then I was on my way home again. That night, sleep didn't take over. Instead I kept tossing and tossing in bed unable to sleep. I think it was past three in the morning when I finally was able to rest but then my alarm went off at six am because I needed to go into my calculus class. I don't know who would dare to get calculous this early for a whole semester. Well that would be me! I got ready, heading towards the kitchen mom decided to stop me.

"Liv, were you able to fix your problems with Christian?"

“No mom! And I’m not going to.”

“Liv, if you mess up your future because of this, don’t come here looking for financial stability. Your dad’s money is not going to last forever. I wanted you to be set financially once you marry Christian but now that you dumped him that won’t be possible. “

“Mom, I don’t care about his money, I am not going to marry anyone to gain financial stability. I can work if I have to but— wait! What do you mean dad’s money is not going to last forever?”

“Well your dad left us a good amount but I’ve been paying your tuition, the house, the bills, and my expenses. I don’t know how long until we do not have any more.”

“Are you kidding me? Your expenses? What are you buying? Is it that brand new designer purse I just saw you with a couple of days ago?”

“Liv, I can do whatever with that money, don’t forget your dad appointed me to be in charge of it! Then once you turn twenty one half of that will go to you.”

“I know, you don’t have to remind me. Well anyways I’m going to need some of that money if I get accepted into the study abroad program. I’ll need it to book my plane and for my stay.”

“Where are you going? I didn’t even know you were leaving?”

“Well It’s not set yet, I’ll find out later today if I’m accepted. If I am, I’m going to Italy to study for six months.”

Mom was not so happy to have to write me a check but she will need to. If not I’ll have to get it from my savings but until I turn twenty one, I’ll have to get the money from her. I’m hoping she doesn’t refuse but knowing she will provide me the money just so I can leave.

“Okay, let me know how much I have to write the check for. Maybe you can get a rich husband in Italy, don’t forget about your mother when you do.” I knew she would write that check, she is a gold digging whore but as long as she doesn’t need to take care of me, she will send me away. I know I shouldn’t talk about my mother like this but she does not deserve my respect. She was always her true self with my father and I, always caring about money more than she did for her family. Bringing my thoughts back, I thanked her then was on my way. Calculus sucked, numbers are not my forte, I hated this subject. After class I went to the library to pass the time until it was time to go check on the list. Time was going so slow, I just wanted noon to come already. By the time it was noon, I walked to the classroom where a bunch of people were already lined up to see if their name was on the list. I waited my turn, closer and closer I got to it then I was there. Checking the list I started to jump up and down because my name was there. My dreams were becoming real, I was about to experience it and it made me extremely proud of myself. I know dad would've been. Professor Dean gave me the list of things I needed to get ready for this trip. The trip was happening in four days. The school has their own private plane but I needed to pay the front office for the trip and the lodge, which they said we would stay in the dorms of the University. I called my mom to tell her to make me the check and to drop it off at the front office. I went home to start packing, feeling fully alive. I danced through the house. Can't believe I am really leaving this place for six months, I'll be a new person when I come back. All I have to think about is my career and forget about everything else. The next day mom had already dropped off the check paying all expenses. Everything was almost ready, packing the most important thing about this trip is my portfolio. Two bags later and I was fully packed. The day of the trip I woke up around four am, took my bags down the stairs and left them at the entrance. Did my makeup and hair, then came to the kitchen to make me a sandwich before leaving. Mom was probably still asleep so I left a note on the refrigerator. I called a taxi to take me to the airport. Once I got there, the one person I did not want to see was there. Christian was standing by the entrance of the boarding gate.

"What are you doing here Christian? Did I not tell you that I did not want to see you anymore!"

"Baby please, forgive me. How come you didn't tell me about this trip? I had to find out from your mom that you are leaving for Italy for six months."

"Well I would've told my boyfriend! If I had one! But since you are not my boyfriend you don't need to know nothing about my life"

"Come on Liv, we need to talk."

"Fuck! Christian, you know I hate that nickname! We have nothing to talk about, just let me go."

"Alright, I'll see you in six months. I hope by then, you'll be able to give me a chance to explain myself and forgive me."

He turned around, walked towards the entrance without turning back then he was out of sight. I felt a little relieved that he didn't want to continue the talk after I yelled. I need him out of my life. I don't ever want to see him again. I wasted two years with this person, I thought he was the one but he proved me wrong. Waiting in the boarding gate, I get a call from my mom telling me that she has decided to also take a vacation but in the Bahamas. No wonder why she kept pressing me to be with Christian. She is wasting money on things that are unnecessary. This trip for me is to set my career up, it's not a waste of money but I guess she doesn't see it that way. The front lady at the gate started calling everyone that needed to board the plane. My chest tightened with fear, this was the first time on a plane, it was also the first time I was leaving the states. New York has always been my home. I love it here, I was born and raised here. Inside the plane the seats were a bit small, I was thankful to have dressed casually because I wanted to be comfortable. The flight was going to be a little over ten hours. I was going to land at the Palermo airport, then a shuttle bus was going to take us to the Palermo University to get settled in our dorms. I was ready to experience everything that is coming my way. I'm hoping my two suitcases arrive on time with my flight. I've heard from other people that have done the study abroad program that the airport sometimes loses people's suitcases. I have my prize possession in those suitcases, my portfolio is in one of them with the rest of the things I need to start the fashion designing program. I haven't really given it a thought about permanently staying in Italy because I love New York but if Italy brings me more happiness, more opportunities for my career, I'll take a chance in making it my permanent home. I can't believe I'm going to Italy in the middle of June which is the start of summer. I was already thinking about the beaches in Palermo. My mind now brings me back to this plane ride where half of the girls going with me were all asleep. I wasn't able to sleep at all, five hours into the plane ride and the plane kept shaking so much. The Pilot kept telling us over the speaker that we should fasten our seatbelts due to turbulence. Six hours went by, no sleep. Then seven, eight, and nine hours of sleep. We were a little under an hour from arriving in Palermo when my eyes started to drift a bit making me take a nap. When I opened my eyes again, the plane was barely about to arrive. I opened my window but couldn't see anything, it was just dark. I look at the time on the screen in front of my seat pointing to seven night time. Then I remembered the time difference between New York and Italy. Once the plane landed, people started getting up from their seats. I was still seated waiting for my turn, with airplane bins clicking shut I kept fidgeting with the lifted skin under my nail. I turned my gaze to the people moving towards the front so I got up as well taking my backpack out underneath the seat. We started walking out but then all of a sudden, I felt the need to pee. During the whole ten hour flight I never got up to go to the bathroom since I was on a window seat and didn't want to disturb the person next to me. The group is all getting together to head over to the shuttle bus. I don't want to interrupt the lady that is talking about the plan to get to the dorms safely so instead I touch the girl next to me and tell her that I need to go to the bathroom. If she could do me the favor of telling the lady to wait for me. The girl didn't seem in a good mood, I guess it must have been an exhausting plane ride for her too. Without looking back I hurry walking towards the nearest bathroom. Emptying my bladder, I flush the toilet, went to wash my hands and check myself out in the mirror which I could see the under bags on my eyes making me look like a raccoon. The under eye bags in my eyes where from the lack of sleep. I put some water on my face then I headed out to join the team but when I got back no one was there. I started to panic because I clearly told the girl to tell the head lady to wait for me. I start pacing around until I see a worker.

"Hey have you seen a big group of people that just landed?"

"Mi dispiace, non parlo inglese"[1] (Sorry, I don't speak English)

"It's okay" waving my hands in a way to tell him I'm fine. I start walking again to see if I can find them but this airport is big and all of them speak Italian. I knew I should've learned the language before coming here. My feet kept going until I was by the entrance doors. I looked left then right, there was no shuttle bus in sight. I'm starting to sweat, I have nothing on me except for my backpack so I start walking towards baggage claim. Once there, I don't see any bags coming from our plane. I tried talking to someone at a kiosk and they told me that everyone had gathered all the bags and taken them to the shuttle bus, mine included. I guess I'll need to take a taxi or something. I go back to the entrance to see if I can find a car that will take me to the dorms but then I see a guy with a balaclava mask just outside the doors. I hurried on my steps to go back inside but it's no help, the guy had already grabbed me from behind putting a rag over my face making my knees buckled then everything after that went dark.

1. Sorry,I don't speak English.

CHAPTER 6

LUCIANO "LUCKY"

Matteo has always been reliable, if he is telling me we have a mole then we have a mole. I don't know exactly how this happened because I cover all of my tracks and all the people we have working for us, have never betrayed us. We need to get to the bottom of this now.

"Lucky, I was at Vitorio's bar for a couple of drinks but I was sitting at the corner of the bar since it was packed. I had my hoodie on for no one to recognize me, I barely had two beers when I heard a bunch of guys on the table behind me talking about "How Lucky doesn't even know that his own people are stabbing him on his back" I tried looking to see if we knew the people that was sitting at the table but I did not recognize anyone, so I did more investigating."

"Okay, people can talk but that doesn't mean it is true Matteo, what other information were you able to find out?"

"I went back to the warehouse to go over all the paperwork, even if I'm not in charge of that section I ended up staying late nights doing my calculation because I wanted to get ahead of anything coming our way."

"How many days have you been knowing this for? How many

nights were you at the warehouse on your own doing this work? You should have told me Matteo!"

"It's okay Lucky, I've known this for about two weeks, I didn't want to stress you with more work so I took it upon myself to do the work after hours. Basically once I got to work on each audit and report, I did find some discrepancies."

"Where did you find the discrepancies? Was it our people? Our imports, exports?"

"Lucky you are not going to like this..."

"Matteo, just tell me! Even if I don't like it, we need to figure out what the fuck is going on!"

"The discrepancies come from your brother's audit from the nightclub and brothel. There are some unexplained amounts of money that are sometimes on the low. Your brother must have not been checking the audit or receipts because someone that works under him is clearly not covering their tracks."

"It can't be my brother! It just can't! I know my brother and I trust him, he would never do this to his own family!"

"Relax, Lucky! I didn't say it was your brother, It has to be someone that is working for him. Your brother probably is trusting this person with the audits and numbers which makes me think he is not double checking his work and they saw a way of messing it up thinking maybe your brother will be to blame not this person directly."

"I have to bring my brother into this, he needs to explain who the fuck is this person!" I head towards Ace's room to bring him to the office. I don't fucking care that he is asleep right now! He is going to give me an explanation about what's going on with the nightclub. I don't even knock, I barge right in waking him up.

"WHAT THE FUCK LUCKY?"

"Get up right now! We need to talk, it's urgent."

"Okay, okay— You could've just knocked on my door before barging in like you own the house."

Ace starts putting on his shirt, then grabs his nicely folded pants that he left on the side chair. I open the door for him to go first signaling to follow me to the office. I tell him to sit down, he is looking puzzled because he can see Matteo sitting down on the other chair beside him.

"Oh this must be something really good or really bad for Matteo to be here at this time of hour!"

"Ace shut up and listen! Matteo is here because he found some issues within our organization and he has brought it to my attention that one of those issues come from the nightclub and the brothel!"

"What the fuck! NO! There can't be issues there! I make fucking sure that everything checks out before handing anything to you. I cover all of my corners to make sure we are not going to get fuck by the "Polizia" (Police) those fuckers come from time to time to check out the place and see if they can find anything illegal to pin it on us."

"Well Matteo ran into some people at the bar saying that we are being stabbed in the back by our own people, so he took it upon himself to go over all the audits, receipts, numbers, anything to do with the organization. What he found out was that your audits and receipts have been a bit misleading. Are you having someone else do this for you? Have you been double checking their work?"

"Lucky— I'm sorry man! I've been really busy with renovations due to some water damage in the nightclub so I had my boy in charge of all the numbers and audits but trust me he is really good and has been working for us for years."

"No Ace! Why— Why would you let someone else in charge of those numbers? We are the only ones that are in charge of those things. Who is this boy of yours? Is he known? Is he trustworthy? Fuck! Dammit Ace!!"

"I get it Luciano, calm down! My guy's name is Luigi Colombo. He has been with us for years working at the nightclub and the brothel. He is good with numbers, I don't even know how he got the audit wrong or what is going on with the audits?"

"Matteo reviewed the audits and receipts and discovered that the discrepancies were primarily caused by a reduction in funds.

Meaning that your guy Luigi either has messed up on the audits or he is stealing money from us."

"What the fuck! No way! That's impossible, he has been doing the audits for some time and we never had any problems before."

"Well that's because we have never really checked in depth until today, if he has been doing them for a long time then we have to go back to the audits and receipts to see if he started doing them right away."

Matteo interrupts our conversation to let us know that he is going back to the warehouse to pull all receipts and check on the numbers from the time Luigi began doing the numbers. Ace tells him the date he started, then Matteo is on his way. I stayed in the office with Ace for a little bit more and I told him not to tell Luigi yet about our findings to just keep an eye on him. I told him to let him keep doing the audits so he doesn't get suspicious. Ace agrees with me then he is on his way back to his room. I touch the back of my neck from all the tension I am feeling. Dad is going to be pissed the fuck off if he finds out so I decided to omit the information until I can find out more about it. I go back to my room to try and catch on some sleep before I get the day started. When I open my eyes, I see the clock on my nightstand pointing to ten in the morning, I barely slept anything. I get in the shower quickly then I'm on my way to the warehouse. When I get to the warehouse I see Matteo in the office, his eyes were bloodshot, he has been up working for weeks and probably getting little to no sleep. As I enter the office Matteo's gaze comes up to look me in the eye.

"So— I was able to find more discrepancies but not when Luigi originally started doing the audits. It took him some months to probably learn the ins and outs and then he started taking them little by little. I do have questions though— Why would Luigi now start making mistakes? Why now? According to Ace he has always been good with numbers. So why now get sloppy? It was just a matter of time until we found out."

"I don't know but thank you for going through all the audits and receipts. Why don't you go home and rest, I'll take over from here. I'll deal with the warehouse stuff today"

"Ring"

"Ring"

"Hello?"

"Lucky, Luigi didn't come in to work today. It's odd because he is always on time and never calls in sick. If he didn't come then that means he already knows that we know!"

"Ace, go find out where you can find him or go check where he is right now so we can pay him a visit"

I hang up the phone, Matteo is eyeing me because he knows what we are about to do. If we are able to find him, I will let him give his explanation but then after he will meet hell itself because I have to make an example out of him in front of all my guys so they know not to fuck with our family. Matteo tells me that he is not going home anytime soon now that Luigi knows that we know. We both head over to the nightclub in my car, when we get there I park my car in the reserved parking space I had Ace make for me. The bouncer outside opens the door letting me in, he knows me enough to know that I am the owner. Inside I find a few girls inside practicing their dances on the poles. It's a little bit after two in the evening so they still have time before we open the doors. One of the girls comes up to me and touches my shoulder to offer me a drink. I know what she is doing but I am not here for that so I tell her to get back to work. When she is back with the other girls I hear her call me an asshole, which is true, I can be one when I want to. I ran up the stairs to get to Ace's office, guiding Matteo to follow me. I open the door of the office without knocking and then find Ace fucking some girl on his desk. The girl screams as we both step out of the office again. This time I knock on the door after a few minutes, the girl already dressed opens the door and walks past me with a smirk.

"Are you fucking kidding me Ace? Why the fuck are you fucking in the office during work hours!"

"Oh come on! I can fuck whoever I want, she was accessible right now and I was too."

"Fuck! Please do that at your penthouse not here! Let's talk business."

"Okay— Okay, I was able to find out from some of the guys that he didn't come because he had something big planned out yesterday. I of course told the guy to not tell him anything about what we talked about or they would regret it."

"That's good okay, did they tell you where you can find him? Or anything about what his big plans were for yesterday?"

"Yeah, they told me that he has been slipping with his tongue asking other people if they want to join him in making money, I asked them if they can give me more information on what the job consists and they told me that they weren't told about that they have to accept and sign some paper in order for him to tell them about his plans. He is trying to cover his ass."

"Fuck! We need to get ahead of this. Can you send one of your most trustworthy guys to infiltrate to get more information?"

"I'm already ahead of you, I sent one of my guys already to do his rounds near his house and then to follow him wherever Luigi goes after that which will lead us to whatever he is planning. He will call me any minute now."

Then the phone literally starts ringing, Ace answers the phone. His eyes widened and I knew it must not be good news. He takes about twenty minutes on the phone talking to his guy before he directs his attention to me.

"You are gonna need to sit the fuck down for this Lucky!"

"Fuck! Just give it to me, I know it's bad either way!"

"Luigi has been stealing money little by little because he has been building a warehouse of his own. He initially received the funds from the payments we make to him for his work. But I guess it wasn't enough so he started stealing our money."

"Did they tell you the purpose of him building a warehouse? Is he stealing our products?"

“No worse, my guy was able to follow him to the warehouse and what he saw!(sighs) It’s something we do not do as an organization, we can deal with ammunition, drugs and money laundering but we have never done human trafficking maybe when dad was around but after you took over, you made sure we didn’t have to deal with human trafficking and most importantly against women and children.”

“Don’t fucking tell me that this bastard is taking women and children and then selling them to the highest bidder? No wonder why he needed to build a warehouse. He is going to need every inch of it if he plans on grabbing a lot of people. What else did they tell you?”

“He says that he already has people in it, he could hear the screams. He is not working alone though, he has teamed up with a few competitors and you are not going to believe who this fucker is working with! The Fucking Romanians!”

“Fuck! Fuck! We need to act now before this gets out of hand! If we don’t do something those poor people are going to end up dead or being sold to who knows who!”

“LUCKY!! If we do something we are going to start a war with the Romanians, we cannot do that. We need to plan this shit out right because we are getting into some tricky stuff.”

“FUCK!

CHAPTER 7

OLIVIA

After everything went black, I hoped everything was just a bad dream but it wasn't. My eyelids felt heavy, when I finally opened them, the first thing I saw was the ceiling. I tried to lift my hand to touch my head but my arms felt as if I had weights tied to them. My tongue was dried, my vision was still blurry. I blinked trying to clear it but the dizziness forced me to close them. The last thing I remember was being at the airport entrance when I saw a person with a balaclava then everything went dark after that. I tried to move my legs— nothing. Panic surged through me, then I heard a door slam. Blinking again, I was able to focus my eyes on my surroundings. The first thing I saw were cages almost like dog kennels seen at animal shelters. My voice came out raspy but soft, the first thing I said was help! But I knew no one was there to help. I looked to my left more cages then to my right, I saw at least ten other women in the same state as me. They haven't fully awakened yet, except for one who was in tears and searching for ways to open the cages.

"Hey— Hey what is it that you remember last? Were you in the same airplane as me? Airport?"

"I was at the Palermo Airport, I was coming from New York for a job opportunity, when all of a sudden everything went dark. All I remember was that I went to the bathroom then after that it went dark."

"What's your name? My name is Olivia, I was coming to study abroad but then I got into this messy situation. Do you think we can find a way to escape?"

"My name is Abigail, I'm trying to find anything I can to try and open the door but I don't see anything. If I have to guess, we are being trafficked. We are most likely going to be here until we are sold as goods, probably drugged, raped, or killed."

"Please don't say that, we need to find a way to get out of here. We have a future outside these walls, maybe we can ask one of the other girls if they have a pin on their hair or something. We have to plan something so we can escape."

"I don't know, I've seen movies about this stuff and they are pretty serious about this. I don't even think we will get a chance to get near the doors."

We both stared at each other in fear. Most of the girls were now waking up slowly, making raspy sounds. That's when we heard the door open. Bloodshot eyes are the only thing I can see, the rest is covered up by a balaclava. This person has gone as far as to cover his hands and neck just in case there are any tattoos. As he is walking towards us I can see that he has some sort of metal stick that looks like a baton. He starts hitting it against the cages to wake everyone up. With a thick accent he starts raising his voice.

"Ladies, welcome to your personal hell! In a few minutes all of you will get ready to have some bloodwork done, everyone will go shower then wear the new outfits that will be provided to you all. Whoever defies my order will suffer the consequences."

Every girl in here are shedding tears hearing this fucker spit orders. I've seen movies of this kind of stuff, the bloodwork usually tells them if we are clean from any diseases. They have us shower and put on the outfits because they will sell us to the highest bidder.

I really hope someone at school knows I never made it so they can start looking for me. Another door opens and we see a group of children crying being led into a large cage. I can understand why they have women but children, that is something I will never understand because they are just children they still have a whole future ahead of them. They are now screaming and crying while the man is yelling at them to shut up. The door opens again, another man with a white coat and no face shield. He starts opening one cage at a time taking blood from each girl. I noticed that he is also injecting them with something, if I can guess he is giving them a small amount of either Heroin, Fentanyl or Cocaine. I am next, sweat trickles down my spine and anxiety is clouding my mind. The doctor opens up my cage, he yanks my arm to get the bloodwork done then uses my other arm to drug me. As soon as it hits my blood stream I can feel it in me, the drowsiness, the nausea and the warmth of it reacting in my body. A few hours go by, opening my eyes I see that some of the girls are no longer in their cages. The door opens up when the same guy with the bloodshot eyes opens my cage.

"Ciao, bella ragazza[1] (Hello, pretty girl) get up, we are going to get you cleaned up."

"No— no please, just let me go! I can give you money please— please."

I don't even see it coming when he strikes me in the face. Yelling in Italian, he pushes me to keep walking forward. Clutching my face from the pain, we stop right in front of a shower stall. I can see some of the other girls naked being told to shower.

"Get naked, you need to shower and get dressed. We have a couple of people coming to take a look at all the girls. You need to be on your best behavior."

I hesitate to get undressed because all eyes are on me, then he pushes me into the cold water and yells at me to get my clothes off again. I start getting one garment at a time, his eyes are all over my

1. Hello, pretty girl

body. I feel violated and embarrassed. I get in the shower rinsing my body from all the sweat. My whole body just feels heavy, skin feels itchy and I feel nauseous. The shower made me a little bit more aware, my face stings from the strike he gave me. He hands me the outfit which is a tiny dress and some high heels. After getting dressed he took me back to the cage, he grabbed my chin tilting it to one side then he cursed at me because now my face is bruised from the strike he gave me. I was taken with all the girls to another room shortly after to be introduced to the buyers. They chose a few of the girls except for Abigail, another girl named Rose and then me.

Another day has passed, no one has come looking for me or any of the girls that have been taken. I don't know where they took the children either. Shortly after opening my eyes from being drugged the children weren't in the cages anymore. It's barely the second day here but I am losing all hope of getting rescued. Tears were falling from my eyes, my heart was in my throat. All I wanted was to go back home. People kept coming in and out of the room they had us. They took Abigail for so many hours, when she came back she was bruised, numbed, with no more tears left to shed. She stopped talking, trauma was taking over her. Disconnected with the world to hide any emotions she was going through. I don't understand why they didn't take me, why did they keep taking her?

"Abigail, Abigail— please tell me you're still in there. What are they doing to you? Please tell me what's going on?"

"It's okay Olivia, I rather they do it to me than you. I don't feel anything anymore, I just let them do whatever they want as long as they don't hurt you."

Her whispered words came out punching me right through making knots in my throat because I couldn't believe she was taking all of the pain to protect me. I wanted to scream, fight and even kill. I want to seek revenge for everything they have done, all the suffering not just for me but for Abigail, for all the other women and children they punished. I prayed for someone to rescue us. It felt like days and weeks had passed by with no connection to the outside world. No one from school has come looking, I was already missing the most important part of my life which is my career as a fashion designer. I lost the opportunity to study and get the certification since I am not there. Even in this moment of vulnerability, I clung to the hope that Christian would come looking for me. He knew where I was going to be staying but I'm pretty sure he won't be coming because I told him to leave me alone.

"Ladies, let's get you guys ready for the new buyers. We have a few other girls coming in today as well so be on your best behavior."

"Please— let Abigail rest, she's been through a lot. She is not feeling well. One of your guys is having all his fun with her and keeps making her disassociate with everyone, she even stopped talking."

"Sorry no! I can't do that! She will need to go through this just like every girl in here."

Bastards, they would not let her rest. She is going to get sick if they keep pushing her to the edge. I needed to do something but I didn't have a plan. It was just hours away from meeting the buyers and I still didn't have a plan. Then all of a sudden an idea came up, I don't know how Abigail will react to it because we were both going to get hurt. Whispering so no one else could hear us, Abigail's gaze went up to look at me.

"Abigail, I have a plan but I don't know if you're going to like this. We are most likely going to get hurt but if we don't try, we will never know. Are you in?"

"What do you want to do? I'll do anything if it means that it gives us more time."

"When the guys open our cage and line us up to head to the shower stalls, I will start a fight. I will have to punch you and you will do the same to me. I noticed that the buyers don't like when we have bruises or are not cleaned up. So are you in?

"Olivia, you are a genius. I promise not to hurt you too badly, but yes let's start a fight and see how it goes from there."

When the guys came in to line us up to guide us to the shower stalls, we did what we said we were going to do. I pushed Abigail, she turned around and pulled my hair to the side and told me to stop being a bitch. I stomped on her foot, pulled my hand back and then struck her in the face. Abigail punched me in the nose, I'm hoping it's not broken. The guys got in between us, they took us back to the cages leaving us for a few minutes alone. After a few minutes the main guy came in and opened both of the cages, grabbing each of our hairs to pull us out. He yelled telling us that we were about to face the consequences. He took us to a dark room, scanning everything I saw: two chairs, a bucket, and a rag. The guys took us to each of the chairs there, they used zip ties to restrain our hands and feet after. At that moment I knew what was going to happen. They were going to waterboard us as a punishment.

"Ladies you are going to experience the torture of your life. Don't ever disobey my rules. Since you guys thought maybe fighting might stop you from getting sold, well it might! But that just means I get to keep you longer, we will get to have our little fun with you both!"

"No— We promise not to do it again, but please don't do this to us."

It was useless because he still threw a whole bucket while our faces were covered with the rag. It felt as if I was drowning, I wasn't able to breathe. He took us back to our cages but not long after Abigail was taken again by one of them. This time I was also taken to a room but this room was different than the rest, this one had a bed. I don't even know the main guy's name but he was sitting down in the middle of the bed. I began to tremble, the fear of being raped kept coming up in my mind. I didn't know what to do. I was exhausted from everything that happened today. There is no way in hell I can fight for my life. This guy was bigger than me and probably way stronger. He got up, then pushed me towards the bed. He lay me down and got on top of me caressing every inch of my body. I was disgusted by his touch, by his smell and by the sight of him. I still couldn't see his face so I made an attempt to take the balaclava out of his face while fighting him to not touch me. He struck me again in the face , busting my lip open. The metallic taste was all over my tongue. I screamed for help as loud as I could even though I knew no one would be coming to my rescue.

CHAPTER 8

LUCIANO "LUCKY"

Matteo had a good point, we do not want to start a war with the Romanians but we cannot let Luigi begin human trafficking because we as an organization decided it was best to just deal with weapons and drugs, not with people. We protect our people. We need to go to this warehouse and burn it to the ground, then I'll take Luigi and make an example out of him in front of the whole organization so people know not to fuck with us. I have to make some calls to the other families to see if they might want to stand with us in case the Romanians decide to start shit because of this.

"Matteo, do you know how many people he has in his possession? I don't care about starting a war! I'm going whether you all come or not. We cannot let him sell these girls or children off to these creeps or pedophiles."

"Lucky, we are all going, you are not going on your own. My contact already sent me the address, we should get going because I don't know how long these girls can hold off. They have been there for a couple of days or maybe weeks.."

"Let's go, call all of the guys to meet us there. Get all your weapons ready, wear your vest and bring clothes for women just in case they need it once we get them out."

"All set lucky, we are taking the van from the warehouse and several of our bulletproof cars."

Getting inside of my car, I make sure I have my gun and my knives that I always keep inside my jacket and on the side of my boot. Matteo gives me the address, then we are on our way. When we get there, we parked a little far out to assess the area and our surroundings. We can hear screams, it's breaking my heart. I could be a piece of shit, an asshole at most but my mother always taught me to respect women. I need to get in there and save them.

"Lucky don't be the hero!, we need a plan before we go in there."

"Don't you hear them screaming Ace! We need to act now before they get hurt."

"No Lucky, listen! We need a plan. Matteo, you have the blue prints of the place?"

"Yes, It was a tight request but my guy was able to send it to my phone. Us three need to go to the back since there is a back door, the rest of us will need to attack from the front. There are no side doors. Pretty much they only have two ways to get out, either from the back or the front. It should be easy if they don't have a lot of people inside."

"I am sending Giani, Carlo and Bruno to the back! Matteo, Ace, Marco, Leone, Romeo, Alonzo, Lorenzo and I will go through the front. If we need more back up Giani please have your walkie talkie on but on your earpiece so you can hear me if I need you to call them."

"Got it boss"

Giani, Carlo and Bruno disappeared to the back of the warehouse while the rest of us walked in unison to the front of the building. We all pulled our guns, kept our earpieces onto the same frequency so we were able to hear each other. We took slow steps to not make any noise, hiding behind some cars we see a person out front making rounds. When the guy turned the other direction, I decided to be fast and creeped up until I was behind him, puncturing my knife in his throat. Blood splattered everywhere, I took his gun strapping it on my shoulder. I signaled the rest to follow me in. Before I stepped inside I put the silencer on the gun as a precautionary measure , then proceeded to go inside the warehouse. Once inside the first thing we see are crates stacked on shelves, Lorenzo opens one to let me know what's inside. He says they have weapons and the second shelf has Cocaine which he probably bought with the money he stole. We keep heading straight until we see two doors, one has a window in front giving us access to see behind it which by the looks of it it's an office and the second door is locked. I am betting the one that is locked is the door we need to go through to find the girls. I whisper into my earpiece for us to go into the second door except for two of my men so they can keep an eye on the other door in case it opens up, they can alert us. I use my knife to break into the locked door, inside I see the cages with girls that have been drugged, not moving. I move in to get started in unlocking the cages to get them out. The lock is impossible to break in with a knife. I have to use my gun but I don't want to make noise. I tell Ace to look for something to muffle the noise to the gun going off. He finds women's clothes in one of the opened cages, so I wrap it around the gun then I pull the trigger. Lucky me! The lock breaks the instant the bullet touches it. I do the same for the other cages to get all the girls out. I don't see children, I am hoping they don't have them somewhere else or worse what if they already got sold? I touch my left, my right and then bring my fingers to my lips to say Amen hoping I'm wrong. I tell Matteo and Ace to help the ladies get outside of the warehouse. I stay behind with Marco, Leone, Romeo, and Alonzo to keep looking around the room to find anything else important. Romeo tells me that there are two opened cages which makes him think that there were two other people there. That's when we hear a piercing scream from a door that is situated on the other side that we didn't even see. Matteo comes back in, saying Ace stayed outside with the girls so he tells Alonzo to go with Ace. Still hearing the screams that are coming from behind the room, I tell Matteo that I'm going in. He stops me telling us to put on the balaclava he made us bring. I do as he says, even though I'm the boss, Matteo knows what he is doing. I go to turn the knob thinking it will be locked but it's not, so I find two more closed doors but in the corner of the hallway there's a guy sleeping behind a table. I act quickly pulling my gun, shooting the guy in the face with my silencer to not give out that we are here. I tell Matteo to go with Leone and Marco to the first door while I go to the other door with Romeo and Lorenzo. The second door is the one where I hear the screams. I count to three then we both kick the door open, the room falls silent. The guy in the balaclava with bloodshot eyes turns around immediately putting his hands up. In the other room I hear Matteo shooting at the guy he found inside. The guy in front of me has no chance because it's three against one. I make the guy lay on the ground, having my guys use zip ties to restrain him. My gaze falls on the naked girl on the bed with a puffy face, blue piercing eyes, and her long silky blonde hair. Sweat making her little hairs up top stick to her face. I move to remove my jacket to place it on her. She flinches when I take a step forward. I speak to her in Italian because I don't know if she speaks English but I can guess she does because she does not look like she is from here.

"Scusate, non sono qui per farvi del male. Voglio solo darvi questo, così potete coprirvi. Voi due! Giratevi!" [1](Sorry, I'm not here to hurt you. I just want to give you this, so you can cover yourself. You two! Turn around!)

"So— Sorry I don't speak Italian. Are you here to rescue us? Sorry —I don't know if you speak English, can you understand me?"

"Yeah I do, I had a feeling you spoke English but I just wanted to make sure first. You're not from here right? But to answer your question, yes, we are here to rescue all of you."

She nods to my question then she leans in to get my jacket, she

1. Sorry, I'm not here to hurt you. I just want to give you this, so you can cover yourself. You two! Turn around!

covers her top half with it while grabbing the bed sheets to cover her lower half. I don't want my guys to see her like this but It's going to be impossible to get this image out of my head. Matteo comes into the room to tell me that we have to go now. One of the girls needed immediate attention at the hospital. I ask her if she needs help walking or if she would like me to carry her. She tells me she needs help because her whole body hurts, everything feels heavy and doesn't know if she can hold her own weight on her feet.

"Alright Blondie, I'm going to wrap you up with the bed sheets to cover you and then I'm going to slide my hand underneath your legs and hold you from your waist okay"

She nods in agreement, making her blush with the nickname I gave her. It suits her and I like it for her. I carry her out of the bed, I tell my guys to grab the fucker on the floor and to put him in the trunk of my car. We were lucky that the Romanians weren't here but I know they will eventually find out and retaliate for taking their partner. I get her inside the car, I go to the driver side to get in. I wait for my guys to go in their car, Matteo has left with the other girl to the hospital in one of the cars we brought in. One of the guys left with the other girls in the van we brought. Alonzo and Bruno are setting the warehouse on fire so they don't think twice on betraying us again. We have three of Luigi's men including him in the trunk of our cars. The rest are dead which eventually will be the future of these men but for now they will remain in the warehouse's basement until we can properly question them. Once the questions are done they will be executed in front of our people as a warning message to everyone that wants to betray us. Once Luigi's warehouse is up in flames, I drive off. I don't know why but I drove to my penthouse, when I got there I carried Blondie out of the car and I told my guys to drive my car to the warehouse to take Luigi and his men to the basement. I told them also to pick me up in about two hours so I can handle everything, I just needed Blondie to feel safe and secure. Once my guys are on their way out of the garage Blondie turns to speak to me,

"Where are we? I thought you were taking me to the hospital. I want to be with Abigail."

I don't know who Abigail is but I'm assuming is the girl that needed medical attention. Matteo took her to his house instead of the hospital to see the doctor we have on call, we usually don't go to hospitals because they always report it to the police. As for the other girls they were taken to the actual hospital. I don't know, I feel very overprotective of this girl. I could've taken her to the hospital but knowing me, I would've been thinking about her the whole time so I took no chances and brought her home.

"Don't worry, you are safe here. They are not going to hurt you anymore. I brought you to my house."

"But— why? Why didn't you take me to the hospital just like the rest of the girls?"

Blondie started to shake, I know she wasn't cold, she was just scared and I get it. She just experienced the most horrific thing in her life. I can't tell her my reasons for why I chose to bring her here but I know it was for my sake but also because she has seen my face. When I put her in the car back at the warehouse all of my guys including me took our masks off so she could see what I looked like. I'm just paranoid she will go to the police and say we rescued her but then that just leaves questions to be asked by the chief police and I don't want to deal with that.

"It's okay Blondie, Abigail— right? She is at Matteo's house being treated by an on-call doctor. I brought you here because I already have an on call doctor on site to take a look at you. Once you start to feel better, you can go."

"Why do you keep calling me Blondie? That's not my name..thank you for rescuing us, I just want to go— wait— what day is it?

"Well you didn't exactly give me your name and since Blondie suits you, I thought it would be appropriate. You're welcome on the rescue part and to answer your question, today is the 20th why?"

"Sorry, my name is Olivia— Olivia Wilder. It's been five days since I got kidnapped. It felt like I was there for weeks, it was horrible, like he said it would be— our personal hell!"

"Nice to meet you Olivia Wilder, my name is Luciano Salvatore but you can call me "Lucky" all of my friends call me that. Who is "he"? Let me take you upstairs to my penthouse so you can tell me how everything happened okay?"

"Nice to meet you Luciano. Okay— let's go upstairs before your arms give out from carrying me."

chuckling at the mention of my arms giving out from carrying her as if she weighs a lot, she is light as a feather. I didn't tell her this but I just smirked and shook my head left and right.

"Okay let's go Blondie, you are too funny."

CHAPTER 9

OLIVIA

I kept screaming for someone to help me get him off me. He was kissing every part of my body, touching it. I knew this would be something constantly in my mind if I was to live. He has not taken the step to sexually abuse me yet but it was just minutes away from it. He lowered his face to my vagina giving it a kiss then came back up to look me in the eye.

"You're about to have the best time of your life. You won't be able to get enough of me after I fuck you so good."

"Please— don't! Let me go!"

Begging for my life was all I could do because he was about to take me either way. But then I hear the door being kicked , three men barging in. They also had balaclavas. Thinking maybe they are his guys, I was wrong because these three men were here to rescue us. I could hear Abigail's scream, hoping that she is also being rescued so they don't touch her anymore. The guy with the hazel eyes points his gun at the guy that is on top of me. He gets up with his hands up, then the other two men do what the Hazel-eyed guy tells them to do, which was to restrain him. I become a little more aware that the three men are looking at me and I am naked. I think the Hazel-eyed guy noticed because he steps forward making me shiver in fear but he hands me his jacket. He spoke Italian to me, I told him I spoke English. He tells me that he is handing me his jacket so I can cover myself. I grab the jacket and pull on the bed sheets to cover the rest. He yelled at the other two men in Italian, I think he told them to turn around to give me privacy because both men turned towards the wall. Once I'm done putting the bed sheet on top of me to cover myself, he took a step towards me.

"Alright Blondie, I'm going to wrap you up with the bed sheets to cover you and then I'm going to slide my hand underneath your legs and hold you from your waist okay"

He had asked me if I could walk on my own but my whole body feels heavy and my legs are going to give out on me. I tilt my chin up and down to give him a nod, giving him permission to carry me. He does what he told me he was going to do and my body is against his hard chest. I could feel his muscles. I can't see his face but his eyes are so beautiful. He carries me out to the car that is waiting up front. I'm set in the back of the passenger's seat, then the Hazel-eyed guy takes his balaclava off, while the other two men follow suit. A smile tugged at his lips because he probably saw how my eyes glittered with lust. This man is gorgeous. His wavy hair, hazel eyes, olive skin and many tattoos from the side of his neck then gets covered by his shirt but if I have to guess this man has tattoos all over his back, chest, shoulders, arms and maybe legs. I turn to face the window once he starts to drive. It took about fifteen minutes to get to the place we were dropped off. He carried me off the car while telling his guys to pick him up in two hours. I kept looking at all our surroundings, nothing looked like a hospital. This looked like a parking lot in a hotel or building but not a hospital parking lot.

"Where are we? I thought you were taking me to the hospital. I want to be with Abigail."

"Don't worry, you are safe here. They are not going to hurt you anymore. I brought you to my house."

"But— why? Why didn't you take me to the hospital just like the rest of the girls?"

He hesitated to answer but he still was a gentleman about it and said,

"It's okay Blondie, Abigail— right? She is at Matteo's house being treated by an on-call doctor. I brought you here because I already have an on call doctor on site to take a look at you. Once you start to feel better, you can go."

There he goes again calling me by that nickname "Blondie". I like it but I wanted to give him a hard time. I introduce myself but I'm hoping he still calls me blondie. He introduces himself, and I can now put a name to his face. I can also stop calling him "Hazel-eyed guy." He is still carrying me all the way upstairs, the elevator feels small with me in his arms. The elevator doors open giving a gorgeous view, his penthouse is on the highest floor, you are able to see the city perfectly. He settles me down in one of the couches in the main living room. Gazing at my surroundings, I'm in awe of this place. Lucky is in the kitchen getting some water and food ready, I have not eaten well in the days that I was taken.

"Lucky.. Can I ask you a question? Please be honest?"

"Yeah, ask me anything you have in mind."

"Am I in any immediate danger? Is that why you brought me here and not to a public hospital?"

"To be honest yes and no— I brought you here because I don't want you being questioned by the chief police, since I was the one that rescued you and you already saw my face, you could identify me and tell them about me. But I don't want people in my business. Look Blondie, I'm not a good person, I'm involved with a lot of bad shit but my mother always taught me to respect women and do what's right. I didn't want Luigi to hurt people by starting to human traffic girls and children."

His response took me by surprise because I wasn't expecting him to be honest. I can tell by his eyes that he is a good person but maybe his line of work is not so much. Luigi is the guy that kidnapped us, I will never forget that name because I want him to suffer. I need to rest and get back up on my feet then make my way to the dorms so I can continue my career.

"If you would have told me to not say anything to the police, I wouldn't have said anything to them about you.. Please don't say you aren't a good person because you are. I may not know you well but you rescued all of the girls including me today, risking your life and the life of the other guys that came with you. You are my hero!— Luigi— is that the guy that took us?"

"Yes, Luigi works for me— well not anymore! He betrayed me and the organization when he decided to steal money from us. I promise he will never ever hurt any other person anymore."

"Thank you, I really owe you my life. Lucky— I'm really tired, I stink and need new clothes. Is it possible for me to use a room to rest, shower and change?"

"Are you able to walk on your own now or should I carry you into my room?"

"YOUR ROOM??"

"Calm down Blondie! My room is the only room that has a private bathroom, unless you want me to set up a different room for you but then that means you have to walk half naked to the bathroom that is situated five doors down."

"NO— Thank you, I'll take your room."

He led the way to his room, showed me how to use the shower since he said it's way different from the states. He gave me some of his clothes because he did not have any women's clothes. Luciano left me in his room the minute he provided me with his sweats, boxers and a plain shirt. The shower was incredible. I used all of Luciano's toiletries, and now I smell like him. However, it's also possible that it was his clothes, as his scent was likely on them. My stomach growled but I was too shy to go to the kitchen at the thought of seeing Luciano there. He is very intimidating and makes me nervous. Opening the door to see if any one was on sight, I tiptoed towards the kitchen. I opened the refrigerator to grab anything to eat, I grabbed ham, cheese and bread to make myself a sandwich. Feeling so comfortable in this kitchen, I pull a stool to eat on the kitchen Island and that's when I hear Luciano in the living room couch say,

"That looks yummy, should've told me that you weren't going to sleep. I could've ordered some food for us."

I turned around lifting my hands to my heart gasping at the notion of him, I wiped my mouth because it was full of mustard .

"Oh my, you scared me. I didn't think you would be here. Are you sleeping on the couch?"

"Yeah, I am. The couch feels more comfortable than the guest room's bed."

"Oh no I'm sorry, I could take the guest room and you take your room back. I wouldn't want to impose."

He starts to shake his head to tell me no but we get interrupted by his stomach growling also. We both got quiet and then started to chuckle. Heading towards the refrigerator again to make him the same sandwich, he gets up to sit by the kitchen island to watch me work my magic, I always loved cooking or anything that had to do with being in the kitchen.

"What are you doing? Are you making yourself another sandwich? Should I order food instead?

"No no, I'm making you a sandwich. Anything I shouldn't put on it? Are you allergic to anything? Nope— don't answer that! I'm so stupid, why would you have something in your refrigerator if you were allergic to it.

"It's okay Blondie, thank you for the sandwich. And no I'm not allergic to anything in my refrigerator, and you are not stupid. I do have a request for the sandwich."

"What's your request?"

"I prefer my sandwiches without any mustard. I just don't like the taste of it. Thank you."

"No problem. Do you know anything about Abigail?"

"Matteo told me that she was treated for all her wounds. The doctor had to inject her with a sleeping serum because she kept screaming, increasing her heart rate. But she is okay for now."

I hand Luciano his sandwich, I lean into the kitchen Island to watch him eat it. He is eyeing me profoundly with those sexy hazel eyes that are making me ache between my legs. I can't be thinking like this, I barely know him. He said it himself, he is not a good person and I do not need to be getting involved in bad situations. I need to call the school to see if they could still take me for the program or if I am out completely.

"Luciano, I need your help. Can you find the telephone number for Palermo University? I was supposed to be in the study abroad program for the fashion designing degree but I never showed up since I got taken away by Luigi."

"You were coming to Italy to study abroad? How old are you? Wait— Where did you come from? Did Luigi give you any clues as to why you were taken? All of the girls we rescued were from the states, no one was from Italy. I need to find out what his motive was."

"Yeah, I'm studying fashion design and got into the study abroad program at Palermo University. I'm twenty years old. I came from New York with a group of girls that were also in the same program, but I got separated from them when I decided to step away from the group to go to the bathroom. Luigi took me from the airport, I don't remember anything after that until I woke up in one of the cages. That's where I met Abigail and the other girls. I saw children there but they were gone the next day. I'm guessing they were sold. He had us showered and dressed sexy to be sold. Some girls did, but Abigail and I weren't sold. I think it had to do with the fact that we were bruised and the buyers wanted the girls cleaned up. Abigail is also from New York. She said she was also taken from the airport. Luigi was grabbing women tourists. That's all I know."

"Wow, that's a lot of information which is really good, thank you. I will question him later today, by the way I will be leaving in thirty minutes, will you be okay on your own?"

"I think so— I'll probably catch up on some sleep."

Luciano stepped up right in front of me, lifted his hand to touch my chin. His proximity made my knees weak, I was trying to catch my breath. My cheeks were burning and I knew he could see because he took a step back.

"Blondie, sorry— Olivia, you are so young, full of dreams. I'm sorry Luigi did this to you. I will make it better, I promise. Don't worry about anything, if I have to talk to your school to let you back in the program, I will. Okay."

"Thank you Luciano, I really appreciate it. I don't know how to re-pay you for what you have done. You are my hero!"

"No, no need. I'm no hero. I just did what my mom taught me to do, treat women with respect and advocate for them when it's needed. Well, Blondie, hopefully I can still call you that but if you prefer I can call you Olivia. You can call me Lucky if you like or Luciano, whatever makes you feel comfortable. I am leaving now, good night Olivia."

"I like it when you call me Blondie, (I blushed) Thank you for everything. Good night Lucky."

It still felt weird calling him Lucky, might just call him by his name.

CHAPTER 10

LUCIANO "LUCKY"

After we took the elevator to my penthouse, I set my room up for Blondie to shower, dress and rest. You could tell she was tired and in need of a shower. Even though she didn't smell from being in the warehouse for a week, she still needed a proper shower to get all the dust and dirt from it. About an hour later Blondie decides to stroll into my kitchen as if it was hers, she opens the refrigerator to make herself a sandwich. She did not see that I was laying down on my living room couch. I decided after all not to go to any of the guest rooms because I wanted to keep an eye out on her and also the beds are not as comfortable as mine. After I startled her and my stomach decides to make an appearance by announcing himself to Blondie with a growl. She moves to the refrigerator again to make me a sandwich. It was the best sandwich I've had in a long time.

Blondie starts telling me all about how she got kidnapped by Luigi, then about the other girls and children. She told me that she came to Italy to study abroad for her career but did not make it to the program because of Luigi. I feel so bad for her because he messed up her opportunities. I told her that I would help her get it back but I don't know if I want to just yet. I told her that my guys are picking me up soon to question Luigi about the whole situation. I wanted to make sure she was going to be okay here on her own.

What she doesn't know is that I have cameras everywhere. I am also locking the door and telling our guy downstairs to keep an eye out on her.

After we say our good nights, I head out to the garage to find Alonzo in my car waiting for me to get inside. We get to the warehouse, Alonzo is telling me everything that has happened in those hours that I was with Blondie.

"Alonzo, where is Giani?"

"Boss, Giani is with Matteo at the moment, he had to go to him because he needed him to buy more medicine for the girl he is with. Giani left me in charge. We tried making Luigi talk but no luck, he is not talking."

"Thank you Alonzo, leave it to me. I will get him talking soon. Find out everything about him. Family, kids, jobs, friends, parents and anything that could help us get leverage on him."

"You got it boss!"

I went to the basement to have a little talk with him but then my phone started ringing. Matteo was on the other end letting me know that Abigail was fast asleep and calm, that the doctor had to put her to sleep. He told me that he will stay with her tomorrow and update me if there are any changes. I asked him about the other girls that were taken to the hospital and he said Giani was heading back to the warehouse to report back on that. We hung up the phone but before I put the phone away, I opened the camera app. I have to check on Blondie. She was fast asleep in my bed looking beautiful with my clothes on her. I put my phone away so it's not a distraction. I enter the room where Luigi is, he looks up at me.

"Look who we have here! To what do I owe the pleasure of you coming to see me Lucky? How are you treating my American lady? Did you fuck her yet? That tiny little body—-"

(Punch)

(Punch)

"Luigi, don't ever talk about her! You piece of shit! Did you rape her? Did you touch her? How many other girls did you sell? Why did you betray my brother and I?

Chuckling and spitting blood from his mouth, Luigi responds back,

"You want to know if I was able to taste every inch of her body? You want to know if I made her come? She enjoyed every second of my cock! I was tired of your brother always bossing me around and not getting the acknowledgement I deserved, so I joined your worst enemies. By the way they will probably be here soon, I suggest to get yourself and your guys ready!"

Fuck! We can't get any rest. I have to call Matteo to get everyone ready just in case, if what Luigi is saying is true. I have to get surveillance at my house and the penthouse, I need to call my brothers so they can be careful. The Romanians don't play about their business. I knew the consequences, now we have to face them.

"Fuck you, Luigi. I'm going to make an example out of you in front of all our people. You should start talking so your death is not painful. I can make it quick and easy if you start talking."

"Fuck you, Lucky! You would never do that for me, I already know I will have a painful death so just get it over with!"

I kicked the door open to leave the basement, passing through the other rooms we have in the warehouse I go into the office. I call my brothers then Matteo and then the guys to get everything ready. Giani got to the warehouse about five minutes ago and gave me all the details about the other girls. I told Giani and Alonzo to get reinforcements here, my home, the penthouse, our other businesses and Matteo's house. We have enough people to make an army. Chaos is going home to be with our father while we settle this shit. Ace is staying at the nightclub like always since we are open until around three in the morning. I check the cameras once more to see Blondie still asleep. I decide to stay here at the warehouse just in case anything happens. I am so glad I decided to stay because not even thirty minutes after I called everyone, The Romanians decided to pay us a visit at the warehouse.

"LUCKY!!"

Someone outside the warehouse is yelling my name, telling me to come out. I get my guys ready, telling Giani to get some guys in the back door and most of them up front with me. I open the door, finding the main boss from the Romanians standing with his guys holding each a gun.

"To what do I owe you the pleasure Andrei?"

Andrei has a very thick accent but I can still understand him. I just don't like that he never asks questions, he loves to shoot first but today is a bit different.

"Ee heard you hav somting dat belongs to me. Vatever it is, we can solve right yes?"[1] (I heard you have something that belongs to me. Whatever it is, we can solve this right?)*

"Look Andrei, Luigi does not belong to you. He was my worker, betrayed my family by doing business with you all. I'm not going to let this slide. I will make him pay. You will not interfere because he signed documents saying he belongs to my organization. He stole money to make his own warehouse and then included you to work together. We are not giving him up without a fight. I don't think you want to start a war between us, right?

He turns around to talk to his right hand man, but can't hear him since he is whispering. He pulls something from his pockets and all my men draw their guns pointing at them. I raise my hands to stop them. Andrei proceeds to tell me he is going to make a call. He must be calling his father. I'm sure they do not want to start a war, we have so many families to back us up and they will ruin their contacts with some of them.

"Lucky! Mee faderr does not vant no warr. Ve vant de money Luigi offerred us. Ve vill go on ourr way once debt has been paid,

1. I heard you have something that belongs to me. Whatever it is, we can solve this right?

yes."[2] (Lucky! My father does not want no war. We want the money Luigi offered us. We will go on our way once debt has been paid.)

"How much are we talking about?"

"He offered us 100,000 Euros to start and told us he would increase the amount once he had a solid business."

"And who are you?"

"I'm the one who deals with the financial side of this organization. You might be wondering why I don't have a thick accent like Andrei, well I was born in Pennsylvania but both of my parents are from Romania, they are also related to Andrei's family making me his cousin. My name is Alexi."

"I'm not going to say nice to meet you because I wish we never crossed paths, Alexi! I will pay half of what Luigi offered you guys and I want all of your people out of my city as soon as the money hits the account."

Alexi turns to Andrei, discussing the information, then he gets on the phone again, I guess his father again. Alexi turns to me again to give me a response.

"We will take your offer, we will provide you the account number but be prompt or we will be back."

"Give my guy the information, you should have your money before you guys get to the hole you all came from."

"Don't be such an ass, Lucky! Be thankful my uncle is being reasonable and does not want a war between us."

Alexi and Andrei walk to Giani to give him the information about the account, then they are on their way. I can't believe this was an easy solution and no one got hurt. I make 50,000 Euros easily with my business, that's why I offered to pay them off. I'm satisfied with the outcome of no war but I won't let my guard down. I'm hoping they don't retaliate later since this was such an easy process. I go back to the basement to give Luigi the news, he is passed out on the

2. Lucky! My father does not want no war. We want the money Luigi offered us. We will go on our way once debt has been paid.

chair that he has been tight up on. I backhanded him, waking him up, he looks up at me smirking.

"I'm guessing Andrei was bought off right?"

"You are right! He didn't care about you. I bought you off for half the price you offered them. Don't think you are worth that money though! You are worth shit but I had to buy you off so I can show my people that you don't fuck with the Salvatore brothers."

"Fuck! Lucky please don't kill me. I'll do anything you want me to do. I'm sorry, I betrayed your family, this organization and the business by making my own by stealing from you."

"It's too late Luigi, you fucked up and nothing and no one will save you. Giani will get you ready for tomorrow."

"No Lucky! What's tomorrow? Please—"

"NO! Luigi! Tomorrow will be your last day on earth. You will suffer a painful death."

I stepped outside the room where Luigi was being held, and I headed towards the office where Giani was waiting for me. I tell Giani to have everything ready for tomorrow, which I want him to have the whole organization here at the warehouse to see the shit show we are about to have with Luigi. Giani nods his head to my requests. I head out of the warehouse to my car to drive back to the penthouse. When I arrived at the penthouse, everything was still dark and quiet. I wanted to go into the room to see her again, see her asleep peacefully but I stopped myself because I didn't want to scare her off. I ended up falling asleep on the couch because I needed to be near her just in case she needed me. An agonizing scream woke me up in the middle of the night. I ran into the room to fight off anyone who was trying to hurt her but when I crashed into the door to open it, she was still laying down on my bed with her eyes closed. She was having a nightmare, the screaming was so painful to my ears. All I could think to do was to wake her up but then I remember what Chaos had told me one day, "you should never wake someone up from their nightmare because they will be disoriented." I decided to go into bed next to her, pulled her into me to keep her close. She stopped squirming and screaming, she hugged me tighter as if she knew she needed me. Her breathing told me she had fallen back to sleep. Unfortunately, she moved so much that she placed herself on top of me, which made it difficult to move or get out. I stayed still, my eyes felt heavy, sleep took over. The next morning I was woken up from my sleep with a slap to the face. I grabbed my stinging cheek, slowly opening my eye lids. With blurred vision, I saw Blondie standing in front of me furiously.

"Why the fuck were you hugging me while I was asleep?"

CHAPTER 11

OLIVIA

Once Luciano left me in his penthouse by myself, I felt really tired. As soon as I laid down in bed my eyelids closed up. I must've slept for a couple of hours. I did feel uncomfortable for a little while, I felt myself sweating and not being able to find my comfort zone even while I was asleep but then all of a sudden, I felt a warmth that made me keep sleeping comfortably. The bright light streaming through the window of the room immediately caught my attention. I cautiously opened my eyes, hoping for a good day ahead. However, my optimism was quickly dashed when I felt the body of another person next to me as I moved an inch. Turning my head to investigate, goosebumps erupted all over my skin. I stood up carefully and slowly to not wake him up. I wasn't mad because I really felt safe with him, I don't know why I felt secure being with him since the very first day. It's hard to explain but to me he will always be my hero and the person that saved me from the monster. I also didn't want him to think this was okay, the first thing that came to mind was not what I intended to do. I raised my hand pulling it back then slapped him.

"Why the fuck were you hugging while I was asleep"

He was touching his cheek, his eye lids opened up but he was speechless. He got up from the bed, walked to the door without answering then he turned around.

"I'll be waiting in the kitchen with breakfast to talk about it."

He left without turning back. I felt really bad because I should've woken him up to ask him to explain but I did something abruptly and now I regret it. I walked to the closet to get the clothes he had brought me yesterday. I was quickly changed and then walked into the kitchen to find him making coffee. I moved to the stool near the kitchen island and quietly stared at his every move. When he was done making coffee, he walked to the refrigerator to get some cut up fruits, eggs and vegetables. He placed the cut up fruit in front of me, gesturing me to grab some. He then grabbed a knife to cut up the vegetables. Once he was done making the food, he placed a plate with some sort of dish that looks like cake.

"Thank you, What's this?"

"I've made my famous breakfast frittata with vegetables, coffee and cut up fruits for you. I hope you like it."

"Smells yummy— look Luciano, I didn't mean to slap you. I was just so confused as to why you were in bed with me. I abruptly acted on my anger without thinking so I'm sorry. Can you explain now?"

"Of course, I apologize if you felt uncomfortable or disrespected. Your loud screaming in the middle of the night frightened me. I took it upon myself to see what was happening, when I went to the room I found you squirming and screaming in your sleep. I knew that you were having a nightmare. I couldn't wake you up because I heard before that you shouldn't do that. The only thing in my mind was just to make you stop screaming so I hugged you and that's exactly what you did. You stopped, hugged me tighter and fell asleep again. Since you were on top of my body and sound asleep peacefully I didn't dare to move. I fell asleep as well until I was woken up with a strike across my face."

"I am so sorry— Luciano, I didn't know. I don't remember

anything about the nightmares. You must have taken them away when you hugged me. I feel so bad now, please forgive me."

Luciano raised his hand to stop me from apologizing. He took my hand in his and told me that he knew I didn't mean to hit him. That made me feel a little better. He held my hand longer than expected without taking his gaze from me which made me nervous. I pulled my hand out his touch and changed the conversation. I asked him if he could take me to the dorms so I can get started with the program. He agreed to take me, but he reiterated his previous warning about discussing the situation with anyone. I crossed my heart to not say anything. We walked to the penthouse's garage, got in the car to be on our way to Palermo University. When we got there, he got out to open my door to lead me inside the main building. As we were walking inside, Luciano is stopped by a man that looks like him only younger. They both hug each other, Luciano turns to me to introduce me.

"Chaos, this is Olivia, she got into the fashion design program here. She will need your guidance to get to the Art building."

"Blondie, this is Alessandro mostly known as Chaos, he is my younger brother. He comes to this University and can help you navigate or answer any questions. Do you think you will be okay with him?"

"Hi, nice to meet you. You look so much like Luciano." I directed my attention to the younger brother then turned my attention to Luciano again.

"Luciano, don't worry I'll be fine, I think I can manage to find it myself but Chaos will be a great help. Go do what you need to do. Anyways, If I start the program, I will most likely be taken to the dorms here. Thank you again for everything, there is no need for me to go back to your place so I guess this will be our goodbyes."

I don't think he liked what I said because his facial expression had changed. I didn't know what he was thinking at the moment. He was speechless and did not take his hazel eyes off me. I grabbed his hand, I thanked him then turned my attention back to Chaos. Chaos could tell what his brother was really thinking because he smirked at him shaking his head. I didn't know what that was about so I asked Chaos if he could take me to the Art building. As I followed him, I felt a growing sense of unease, each step taking me further away from Luciano. I kept turning around to look at him. With each step I took, his brows kept drawing together, and he shrugged his shoulders. I felt as if he wasn't ready to let me go or still wanted to say something to me but I cannot rely on him, I need to do this on my own. Chaos guided me to the art building and told me if I needed anything to come looking for him at the business building, that he would be there all evening. Being brave I stepped inside the art building, I went inside the main office to talk to someone that might know about the program. A very nice lady sat me down and told me to wait for a counselor. Once inside I explained my situation. The counselor was horrified by the things I told her I went through. She proceeded to tell me that since I didn't appear for a whole week, that they gave my spot to someone else. They put my suitcases in storage until I would come to claim them. I tried everything I could even go as far as to call professor Dean to see if he could do anything on his end. He told me he couldn't, that he was sorry for the unfortunate events that transpired but the program was very strict. They needed to fill in my spot. Since I didn't have a spot anymore in the program, I wasn't allowed to stay at the dorms either. I did not have anywhere else to stay. I didn't have access to money to buy a ticket back to the states since my backpack was taken by Luigi. The only thing I have is my suitcases with my clothes, my portfolio and some other toiletries. My brain at the moment was foggy, I couldn't think straight. Left the art building with two of my suitcases towards the business building. It was way past evening time, hoping to still see Chaos but he was long gone by the time I got there. I was so scared, lonely and stranded. I didn't have anywhere to stay or available money to pay for a hotel or a taxi. I went back into the business building. I know Luciano is known here due to his organization so I started asking people around. Lucky enough I was able to interact with a guy named Luca, who told me he knew Alessandro "Chaos". He took out his phone from his pocket to dial someone. On the other end muffled sounds but Luca kept saying okay and yes the whole time. I was getting desperate. When he hung up he told me that Lucky will be coming soon to pick me up. I got so excited because I was no longer stranded. I was not going to end up alone sleeping on the streets. Luca waited with me outside the building for Luciano to come pick me up. A black Escalade made a stop in front of us then Luciano got out of the driver's side, dressed up in all black. His hair was damped as if he just took a shower. He smelled like cinnamon from his cologne. Luciano stood in front of Luca telling him something I couldn't hear then Luca got in his car and left. He turned to me, all the happiness I felt to see a familiar face made me blush. I quickly ran to hug him, breaking down at the moment my skin touched his. He hugged me tighter, kissing my forehead, telling me that everything was going to be okay. Opening the door of his Escalade, I went inside waiting for him to load my suitcases in the back. He got into the driver's side quickly, interwinding his fingers with mine, he stared at me for a little while trying to read my facial expression. I was too tired to give off any vibes, he continued to drive us home. "Home" that's how it feels to me since the first day he brought me there. Once there, Luciano carried my suitcases guiding me to follow him to the elevator. We got to the top of the penthouse setting the suitcases in the main entrance, he turned to me.

"Luca told me that you were in distress when you were asking people around if they knew me or my brother. I should've waited for you or given you my number to call me. I'm sorry."

"No, don't worry, It's okay. I just didn't think that they weren't going to accept me in the program. I had a feeling that once I told them the situation, then I would be still given the opportunity but they gave my spot to someone else. I didn't have any money on me to call for a taxi or to get a ticket to fly home, Luigi had taken my backpack when he kidnapped me. I am sure it is still in the warehouse."

"Sorry Blondie but the warehouse is no longer there. You might not remember but we burned it down."

"Oh no, I forgot about that. I'll need to call my mom to send me some money so I can fly back home."

"I could give you the money, If you don't mind."

"No— My passport was also in the backpack. I will never be accepted back into the states without my passport. Thank you for offering. I will need to go to the Embassy to see if there is a way to apply for one or something."

"In the meantime, you can stay here. I don't mind having you here but I will need to set up one of the guest rooms because my room has the comfiest bed and I need my bed back, okay."

"No worries I can take another room. I do have to agree your bed is like clouds. Thank you again Luciano for everything you have done for me."

After our conversation, I went to the guest room closest to the kitchen. I went to take a shower and forgot what Luciano had told me days earlier that I would have to walk in a towel from the bathroom to the room. The walk of shame came once I was done showering but was more embarrassing was that as I was running to the room, I hit a wall. Not just any wall, It was Luciano's hard chest that I collided with. He looked down on me, feeling my still damped skin and his. He had also showered. We both looked at each other " I'm so sorry" we both said. We both passed by each other and went inside of our rooms. Embarrassed at whatever just happened, I didn't want to go into the kitchen just in case he was there but my stomach kept telling me I was hungry. I tiptoed to the kitchen to make myself another sandwich but this time Luciano didn't come out of his room. When I got done eating, I brushed my teeth and went to sleep.

CHAPTER 12

LUCIANO "LUCKY"

I felt my body heating up at close proximity, I touched her damped skin and my body felt a tingling sensation, fluttering in the pit of my stomach and I don't know if she saw it in my face because I was red as a tomato. I cannot feel anything for Olivia. She is too young for me, she has a future for herself and I am not included in those plans. I am too busy with our family organization, I am old, and not a good influence on her. After we both were inside of the rooms, I laid in bed awake for hours just contemplating life and day dreaming of her body. My hand slid down my body at the hems of my boxers. I continued to slide it down until I touched the massive hard-on I had. I needed a release, if not I was bound to have blue balls. I stroked my dick slowly then increased the speed until I exploded my cum all over my hand. Got up to clean myself then went back down to sleep. My tired eyes shut off for hours until I heard the floor creaking, my door opened up slowly. I didn't think twice, I was quick. I grabbed my pistol from under my pillow aiming it towards my door but I stopped myself when I saw Blondie there. Puffy and teary eyes were all I saw. I immediately got up to wrap her in a hug, she hugged me back.

"Are you okay, what's going on? Have you been crying? You scared the shit out of me, I almost shot you!"

"Sorry Luciano, I don't know what I was thinking coming into your room. I just needed you. The nightmares are back. I woke up crying and scared. All I wanted was to feel safe— you are the only one that makes me feel safe. Can you stay with me until I fall asleep?"

Cupping her chin, I gave her all my attention. I hugged her tighter because I just wish to take all her pain away but those nightmares are something I can't control. I used to control everything that surrounds me but with her nightmares I can't and it's killing me.

"Don't worry, why don't you stay here with me. My bed is bigger than the one in the guest room. I'll carry you to your bed once you have fallen asleep okay."

She nodded silently, and I led her to my bed. I pulled her into my chest, hugging her tightly as I could. Her shallow breathing indicated that she was fast asleep. I passed out for a while and then carried her to her room. I walked back to mine, falling asleep again. The next morning I woke up to the smell of coffee. I swiftly headed to the bathroom to brush my teeth, apply some cologne, and straighten my wavy hair. Upon entering the kitchen, I was surprised to find her in the tiniest shorts and tank top, joyfully dancing as if yesterday's nightmare had never occurred. I startled her when I sat down on the stool by the kitchen island. She gasped turning to me then smiled at me. She place a cup of coffee with cut up fruits in front of me.

"I hope you like what I made. This is something we eat in the states. Eggs, bacon and pancakes. I had to ask the main lobby to deliver the ingredients because you did not have much in the refrigerator. I also told them to charge it to the penthouse— hope you don't mind."

"Not at all, you can order anything you want. I should stop by at the store to get more things since we are now going to be sharing the space. This smells amazing, it reminds me of when I was in New York with my mother."

"Have you been to New York? Is that how you know English? Wait— I just realized that I don't really know much about you but you know more about me, we need to rectify that!"

"My mother was born in New York, she took my brothers and I there when she was still alive. She would talk to us in English all the time and then my dad would talk to us in Italian. We learned both languages fluently. What do you want to know? I'll try to answer all of your questions."

"Okay, I meant to ask you your age but I didn't want to make you uncomfortable by asking that."

"Blondie you can always ask me anything you want to ask even if it's difficult to answer, I'll try my best to always be honest with my responses. Now going back to your question; I am thirty three years old, I know I'm old."

"No— you are not old! You are just more experienced and mature."

Blondie seemed to not mind my age since she was smiling at me when I responded to her question. I was a bit scared of telling her my age because she is so young, I don't want her to think I want to take advantage of that. I genuinely care for her. I don't know how it happened but since the first day I saw her, I became very protective over her. It was as if there was a sign from above to look after her. I might also like her a lot, that's why I was devastated yesterday when I dropped her off at the University and she told me she would be okay on her own. When she turned to leave, I couldn't keep my eyes off of her, she was leaving me, didn't know if I would get to see her again but I am so glad she came back to me.

"Do you have any other questions for me?"

"Yes, actually. What is it that your job consists of? Where in New York have you been to? And why aren't you married with kids?"

"Wow there Blondie, that's a lot of questions, let me go one by one but you do know I can't really tell you the real information about what I do for a living right? — Well my father stepped down from the family business passing it over to my brothers and I. I am the head boss for most of our business while Ace is in charge of the nightclub. "Chaos" is just focusing on school. In New York, I've been to Manhattan, Brooklyn, Williamsburg and The Bronx. Now to answer your last question, I've never really thought about getting married or having kids because I'm always busy with the job. I also don't want anyone to be put in a dangerous situation for being with me."

"Luciano, I'm so sorry if I overstepped by asking the last question or if I made you feel uncomfortable. I can't believe you run all of your family businesses, did you do this since you were young? I'm also baffled that you know a lot about New York. I'm from Manhattan, I have also been to all those places you mentioned. New York is beautiful, it has been my home since I was born and it has the most important memories of my dad."

"When are you going to stop calling me Luciano and start calling me "Lucky" I feel like I'm in trouble every time you call me Luciano. The only person who ever called me that was my mother which was whenever I was in trouble. Other than that she would call me Lucianito. My mother's family comes from Lima, Peru. She spoke three languages, but her favorite was always Spanish. Even when I was older, she would emphasize the last letters of my name to remind herself that I was still her baby. You can call me whatever makes you comfortable though. So tell me more about your father."

"Aww that is so adorable, maybe I should call you Lucianito!"

"Well, my father was my first love, he was a very loving father. He gave me everything I needed in life. He provided for me financially, gave me a lot of love with actions and words. The worst day was when he came up to me one day letting me know that his doctor had told him that he was sick and needed a lot of consultations and exams. I would accompany him to most of them then in one of them the doctor had given him his diagnosis letting him know that he had cancer. His health declined fast, he started feeling sicker and sicker even with radiation and chemotherapy until he lost the battle, replacing that day as the worst of my life."

I seen Olivia cry before but not like this, with so much emotion. I can tell that her father was her favorite person. I wish I could have met him. He sounds like a person I would've enjoyed time with. I stepped in front of her tilting her chin up, her piercing blue eyes looked me in the eye and we had a moment of silence as if we were paying some sort of tribute to her father. I hugged her after swiping my fingers across her cheek to catch the tear she had shed. I kissed her forehead, which was quite intimate for me, and I could tell she got really nervous and flushed. I stepped away missing her presence the minute I pulled away from her. I ordered some food for us, we ate burgers since Blondie had said she was missing home. That was the first thing that came to mind about American food. We both laughed when the food was delivered because she somehow knew I was going to order this. After finishing our burgers we sat down on the couch turning on the TV. She turned to me and said she didn't understand any Italian. I told her to not worry because the TV cable I have has shows in English. We put on a movie she chose, of course it had to be a romantic movie. After an hour of watching the movie, I fell asleep. I opened one eye to see if she was still watching but to my surprise she was laying on my shoulder asleep as well. I didn't dare to move because she looked so innocent, such a beautiful angel. *What am I thinking? I cannot think like this. She is vulnerable right now and I need to take care of her until she gets back on her feet.* I carried her to her room, gave her one last look then I walked out of there. I would've thought she would wake up screaming again but she didn't this time, she slept peacefully all night. The next day I woke up to her again in the kitchen making breakfast. I had already showered and dressed. Blondie placed a plate and coffee right in front of me but she had a look on her face that I couldn't read.

"Lucky, I want to be productive. Maybe I can get a job or something. I also have to fix the thing with my passport. Can you drop me off at the embassy?"

"You called me "Lucky" I'm honored. Also NO to the job, I can give you money if that's what you need. I'll have someone take you to the embassy, I'm needed at the warehouse right now so I'll be living soon."

"No Luciano! I need to do something to keep myself busy. I don't want your money!"

"Okay, okay— I get it but you can't be working out there when people know that you are staying with me, I have a lot of enemies and I need to keep you safe."

"I understand, I'll see what I can do to make myself busy. Are you working all day at the warehouse?"

"Why don't you work on your designs? Maybe you can find another program that can take you and yes, I'll be all day at the warehouse. I have not been focused on it since I was here with you but I am needed now, I cannot cancel my meetings."

"You are right, I need to get started on my portfolio. I will do some research on other programs that might be able to take me."

"I'll have Giani take you to the embassy to get your passport processed. I got you a phone, I have put my number and my brother's numbers on it just in case you need us for anything okay."

"Thank you Lucky, I am grateful for all your help. I'll see you later?"

"Don't wait up, I might be here past midnight. I'll definitely see you tomorrow."

I felt some type of way of leaving her again but I couldn't keep telling my people that I couldn't go for personal reasons. I need to show up for my meetings with all the clients that are paying for their shipment. I thanked her for the delicious breakfast, then left. I sent a message to Giani to take Olivia to wherever she needs to go. I am really hoping that this passport issue takes longer than usual so I can have more time with her. I'm afraid that if she gets an expedited passport that she might leave back to the states where I'll probably won't ever see her again.

CHAPTER 13

OLIVIA

Luciano left to work, he has been with me these past days and hasn't paid any attention to his work. Today he got changed and let me know that he is needed back at work, he left as soon as he finished breakfast. He reminded me to work on my portfolio, I didn't even remember about it since I haven't been thinking about that after getting kidnapped. Luciano does not want me to work because he thinks I'll be exposed to his enemies. Giani picked me up to take me to get my passport resolved. They told me that I had to pay a fee and I would need to wait a couple of weeks. Giani was told by Luciano to pay for whatever fee they charged me and he provided the penthouse address to get it delivered. Giani took me back to the penthouse, once he left me there I got my portfolio out of my suitcase and I began to design more things that I had in mind. I didn't even see how long I spent on my designs but it must've been hours on it because when I started it was day time and now it was night time. I looked at the phone Luciano gave me this morning. My hands were itching to dial him but I didn't want to bother him. Another hour has passed, I'm starting to miss him too much. I don't know what is going on. This whole week has been a learning experience because I learned that his close proximity makes me happy and nervous. I learned that every time he touches me even if it's not intentional or even just a hug makes my stomach flutter, my knees weak and makes my heart skip a beat. I learned that I am able to sleep better when he is next to me and lastly I learned that I am starting to catch feelings for him but he has pointed out before that he is not a good person, that his job takes him away from the people he loves and he doesn't want a relationship while him being in charge of his family business because of the risks people go through when they are close to him. I don't want to make the wrong decision, I just ended a two year relationship with Christian and I don't want Luciano to think I want to be with him as a rebound. I continued drawing my designs but stopped abruptly once more because my mind couldn't focus anymore, all I could think was why can't I just follow my heart and be happy. Why can't I just be with Luciano? Why does everyone want to tell me what to feel or what to do? My mother tells me what to do, Christian tells me what to do, Anna kept telling me what to do. I am so tired of everyone telling me what I can't or I can do. I grabbed the phone, dialed his number. It only rang once before he answered.

"Olivia, are you okay?"

"Yes— I am why wouldn't I be?"

"Because you are calling me and it's late, have you seen the time?"

"No, I was working on my drawings, the time was not in my mind. Sorry, am I bothering you? I know you are work—"

"Blondie, you are never a bother. I'm glad you called, I just got out of a boring meeting and hearing your voice made it all better. I'm getting ready to leave soon. Have you eaten?"

"No, I forgot to eat since I was re-designing my portfolio. It's okay though. I can make myself a sandwich then go to bed."

"I'll grab something on the way home, maybe we can watch one of those movies you like if you are not too tired."

"That actually sounds perfect. Can't wait."

I went to shower after we ended the call. I was so excited to see him that I didn't even care if I was tired or not. Not even thirty minutes passed, Luciano was walking out of the elevator with bags in his hand. As soon as he entered the kitchen I could smell the delicious food. He brought Italian food which is my favorite by the way, he didn't even know that but it's my comfort food. My father would always take me to this little Italian restaurant in Manhattan any time he knew I needed it. Luciano grabbed some plates then served the food. We headed to the living room, we sat down to enjoy our food and the movie I had chosen. After we were done with the food, Luciano and I got closer to keep each other warm. He placed his hand on my shoulder and I placed my hands around his waist. This to me was very intimate but I didn't care. I was hoping he would take the next step but I know he won't. So I looked up to him, eye to eye we kept our gaze until he lowered his face as if he was going to kiss me. I closed my eyes waiting for his lips to touch mine but it never came. I opened my eyes, he was still staring at me. I felt some type of way as if he was rejecting me. I started to move away from him but he stopped me by placing his hand behind my neck then pulled me onto him. His lips were on mine, kissing me fiercely. His other hand came up to my neck squeezing just a bit, not to the point of cutting my air. This was more as if he was letting me know he was in control, I like it, I didn't even know that was something that would turn me on. The kiss didn't last long because the phone interrupted us. We pulled away, he had the biggest grin and I didn't know how to breathe. As Luciano is picking up the phone, he gets up frowning his eyebrows. His mood had changed, I got up with him but I stayed in the same place. He hung up the phone then turned to me.

"Do you know a Christian Knowles?"

Oh no, how does he know of his existence? I was really hoping that this would be a joke but it wasn't because he was mad, big mad!

"Yes I know him, why?"

"I didn't know you had a boyfriend back home! Why didn't you say anything? You let me kiss you and still didn't say anything. How could you lie to me, I've been nothing but good to you!"

I am already shedding tears because he wasn't letting me talk or defend myself. He was just raising his voice not letting me explain anything. How does Christian seem to just mess up everything for me? He messed up my relationship with my best friend and now with Luciano.

"Luciano— Please let me explain, If you just let me talk please.."

"Fine you have two minutes because your "Boyfriend" he is downstairs waiting on my call to let him up,"

What the fuck! What is that idiot doing here, there is no fucking way he came from New York to Italy. This had to be a joke. Last time I saw him I told him to wait until I came back to talk. Now he is here messing my life again.

"Look I didn't say nothing about Christian because he is not my boyfriend, well not anymore, he cheated on me with my best friend and I decided to take the opportunity to study abroad to run away from my problems but to also start up on my career. I told him before I left that we were done, I swear! I have no idea why he would be here."

"He really cheated on you with your own best friend?"

He pulled me in for a hug, apologized for raising his voice.

"Yes, I found her in his apartment having sex. You know what's funny, she never liked him. She always talked shit about him, I don't know how she decided to have sex with him."

"Do you want me to tell the concierge to not let him up?"

"We have to talk about everything that happened, I never had the chance since I had to leave for the program and I had told him that I would talk to him once I got back so I think he deserves for me to listen to him but I am not changing my mind about him, you don't have to worry. Can you give me like ten to fifteen minutes with him?"

"Okay but I need to meet him face to face then I can go to my room. Just so you know I will be hearing everything just in case okay."

"That's fine."

Luciano dials the concierge to let him know he is allowed to come up. As soon as Christian walked out of the elevator, he ran to me to hug me. I felt as if I was losing air, so I shoved him off me. Luciano took a good look at him and then nodded at me letting me know he was going to the room.

"What are you doing here Christian? How did you find me?"

"Oh my sweet Liv, I thought we lost you or something. What happened to you?"

"Christian answer me! How did you find me?"

"When you left, not long after Anna got a call from the program telling her that she needed to take someone's spot since they could not find that person. She called me to let me know, then she was put on a plane here to start the program the next day of her arrival. She called me again to let me know that you were the person that was missing, she was the one who took your spot. I had to make arrangements for the games at home with the coach but he told me I needed to play at least the two home games and then I was allowed to go. I took the first plane, then went straight to the university. Anna told me that some people had seen you with a very known gang member, I paid someone to tell me, now here I am."

"What the FUCK! Anna took my spot! She is here? In Italy? I can't believe it. I never saw her when I went to pick up my things. Anyways, why do you care? We are done, not together Christian!"

"Liv, I still love you and I was worried about you. I told your mom I would come to find out what happened to you. To my surprise I found out that you are living with the most dangerous known gang member of Italy!"

"Christian, stop calling me Liv, and fuck you! You never loved me! If you loved me like you say then you wouldn't have cheated on me with my best friend. Don't make it seem like my mom was worried because she never called me or the school to ask for me."

"Olivia it was a moment of weakness, everyone has those. I'm sure you've had that with this guy in here!"

"Stop! You are the last person I need to tell my business to. Luciano is my business, If I want to be with him then I'll be with him.

I don't care what people say about him because he has shown me who he is."

"Olivia you can't be for real! He is dangerous! He is not even your type!"

"You don't know what you are saying. You don't know my type."

"Yes I do, I am your type, I've always been your type."

"You were my type Christian but that's in the past. I can do whatever the fuck I want because I am in control here. Please leave! I am not going back home yet and I don't need you taking care of me! It is not your job! Not anymore!"

Luciano must have seen how frustrated I must have been because he came out of the room telling Christian to leave. Christian did not move an inch, Luciano stood in front of him, no care in the world. Christian announced out loud that he was not leaving without me but Luciano was a few inches taller than him. He stood with his chest out, telling him that he was not going to let me leave with him. I got in between to tell Christian to leave but Luciano grabbed me by the arm pulling me behind him. He raised his voice again telling him to leave, making Christian turn to the elevator to leave. He turned around saying that he would be back as he was entering the elevator. Luciano took a step forward trying to reach him before the elevator doors closed but I stopped him by pulling him by the arm.

"Luciano stop please— don't make it bigger than what it is. Let him go, he is no longer important to me. It's late, we should go to bed."

I start walking to my bedroom but then I feel him right behind me. All of a sudden I'm being swept off my feet being carried away from my room.

"Hey— what are you doing? Lucky?"

"Blondie, I am not letting you go to your room. We are finishing what we started, we are not done yet."

CHAPTER 14

LUCIANO "LUCKY"

I am done hiding my feelings, she needs to know how I feel about her. The way her blue eyes just keep staring at me, it's making my heart all weak. We decided to eat and watch a movie but then she got really close to me and I put my arm around her shoulder. She then looked up but wasn't saying anything. I think she knew I wasn't going to make a move because she decided to pull away but I was not going to let my fears take me away from her. Olivia is the first girl that has ever made me feel this way. She has my heart, I knew this since the first day I saw her but then all the little things like spending time, the close proximity, the smell of her, her smile and everything that involves her. I realized I couldn't deny it any longer when I kept looking back at my phone today at work, as if I was just waiting for her to call. When I saw her number appear on my phone, I instantly forgot about everything at work. She lit up my bad mood. I didn't want to deny myself love anymore, I have done it for many years of being the caretaker of every one that needs it; the job, my brothers, and my father. It's time to make my own decision. Before she could pull away, I put my hand behind her neck to stop her. She closed her big blue eyes, I could hear both of our heart beats.

I'm going to risk it all, I hope she reciprocates her feelings for me. Before she could say anything my lips were on her. I was hungry for her, her luscious lips were perfect for mine. She tilted her face to the side to deepen our kiss, I felt her tongue and mine connect. The fucking phone started ringing breaking our kiss apart. The concierge called me because there was someone outside wanting to come up. I didn't recognize the name of the person but then I heard the guy say to ask for Olivia, then my mood changed completely. I got furious, she could see it. I asked her if she knew a Christian Knowles, her facial expression changed as well. She knew him and didn't mention him at all. When the concierge said to me that he was her boyfriend, I felt as if my world was caving in.

"I didn't know you had a boyfriend back home! Why didn't you say anything? You let me kiss you and still didn't say anything. How could you lie to me, I've been nothing but good to you!"

She tried to explain herself but I didn't want to hear it at the moment. I was pacing the living room until she stopped me and said my name. She said "let me explain please" with tears in her eyes. I knew that I needed to hear this. She told me everything that went down with her, Christian and her ex best friend. I'm glad I let her explain because all of this was already clouding my mind with bad thoughts. Who in their right mind would cheat on Olivia, she is smart, funny, hot and a really nice person. Christian fucked up and he knows it, if not he wouldn't be here wanting her back. When Christian entered the room, I could tell that he was an asshole. He is not taller than me but he kept puffing his chest as if he was trying to show off that he is bulky and I am not, well I am all muscle and taller than him but he is not intimidating me. As soon as I turned to Olivia, she gave me a nod letting me know it was okay to go to the room to give them space to talk. I pulled up the camera that is in the living room watching them. I can tell that Olivia is uncomfortable because she is keeping her distance and keeps playing with the hem of her shirt. When he gets closer to her to tell her that he is her type, I was about to throw my phone towards the wall because I cannot picture her with anyone else. He is making me furious. I just want to go out there and punch him in the face or worse; put a bullet in his brain. I couldn't contain myself anymore, I walked out the room finding him getting closer to her. I got in between telling him to leave then Olivia got in between both of us. I pulled her behind me again, raising my voice telling him to leave. He raised his voice at me as well telling me he was not leaving but Olivia got in between again yelling at him but when I said leave now he started walking towards the elevator saying that he would be back so I started walking toward the elevator to stop him but Blondie pulled me saying to stop. Once he is out of sight, Olivia says that it's late and we should go to bed. Ohh no! She is not going to avoid what happened before we were interrupted. I will finish what we started. As she's walking to her room, I fasten my step to carry her. She gasps to tell me what the hell am I doing. I tell her that she is coming with me. I carried her into my room, laying her on my bed. Blondie's blue eyes were connected to mine. We were quiet until I broke the silence by telling her that I wanted her in bed with me, that she wasn't allowed to go to her room.

"You can't keep me prisoner in your room Luciano"

"I am not, I just want you here. I sleep better when you are with me, plus I want to have a chance to finish what we started before we were interrupted by your ex."

"Oh yeah? What is it that you want to do?"

"I want to tell you how I feel about you but I'm afraid that you don't share the same feelings or that you might think I'm too old for you. I've been holding back on my feelings for you because you are so young and have a future for yourself. I don't want to be selfish and keep you here. I also don't want to put you in any danger—"

"Shh— Luciano, let me start by saying that I never really thought of you in any way at first because I just had gone through a traumatic event. As we spent time together and I saw the real you, you made me start feeling little things here and there. I actually realized that I been doing what everyone else wants and never really had a chance to choose for myself but today when you told me you would be gone all day at work, something in me made me realized that my feelings for you weren't just to be thankful but because I actually find you attractive, you make me feel safe, I enjoy time with you and I really missed having you with me all day today."

Hearing her say all this to me made my dick stirred inside my pants, I've never really had feelings the way I have them for her. I am scared for what this might bring because I know I have enemies, when they see that she is my weakness they will use it against me. I have to have a plan in motion if we want this to work.

"Look Olivia, I just want to be one hundred percent transparent with you on how our relationship could look if you decide to be with me. First people will talk because of our age gap, I am thirteen years older than you. If we are willing to undergo the judgement of the people then we should be okay. You will need to get used to having security and people with you all the time because I am not willing to risk your life for nothing. You will need to know that you cannot work, or be on your own anywhere you go, I have too many enemies."

"Wow, are all those rules to be with you? Lucky I will feel like a prisoner. I need to be able to do something, feel productive. I cannot just stay in your home all day without doing anything. I want to be an independent person. I wasn't raised to be treated like a queen even as much as it sounds like it's great, I cannot just stand here and not do nothing. We would need to come to some sort of an agreement. I am willing to try but there's got to be something we can meet in the middle right?"

"No, I will not play with your safety Olivia. You are either in or out. I cannot lose another person in my life."

"God, you are intolerable. You really think my life would be in danger if I am with you?"

"Yes Olivia, I am the top family mob boss in Italy. I have too many enemies. I wouldn't dare to tell you all of this, if it wasn't true but it is."

She is quiet, thinking about all the things I just mentioned to her. I know she will probably say no to this because she is too independent to stay tied down to someone who will only bring her trouble. I don't really want to think about her leaving me. I think I have fallen in love with her. I won't tell her because it's too soon and might scare her with my sincerity but I am head over heels for this girl. She has been driving crazy since the day I brought her here to my penthouse but if I am being realistic I think It was her blue piercing eyes that captivated the moment I saw her at Luigi's warehouse.

"Luciano, I really want this to work out. Maybe we can come to an agreement about the little things but I also don't want to feel like a prisoner."

"I understand, we can talk about it more but I would really like to just kiss you right now."

"Then kiss me Luciano because I really want you to kiss me right now too."

I kissed her softly, laying her on my bed. The heat was increasing with every touch. I love the taste of her lips. I was already on top of her kissing her cheeks, neck then went back to her lips. My dick stirred in my pants wanting to be freed. I know she felt it because she pushed her hips up. I needed to stop because I wanted our first time to be memorable and comfortable for her.

"Baby, I need to stop because if we don't, I will take you right here right now."

"Then take me please— I want you!"

"No, I want to take you on a proper date first and get to know you before we go further."

"Wow, you're such a gentleman. I love it."

"Do you want to stay here or do you want to go back to your room?"

"I want to stay here. I feel better when I'm with you."

"I love the sound of that, then let's go to sleep. Tomorrow is a big day. Tomorrow is Luigi's judgement day. I have been extending this day because I have been busy with other things but this cannot wait any longer. I have to let everyone know what he did and what could happen to people if they betray me."

"Can I be there? I would really like to be there to get some closure on what he did to me."

"I'll bring you along but you will not be present when he dies because I don't want you to see me differently. This can change you as a person and also change the way you look at me, I won't expose you to that."

"Okay, that's fine. Do you know how Abigail is?"

"Abigail is still at Matteo's house. She is still recuperating, she had more wounds and trauma done on her and she is slowly making progress but she's been having nightmares, severe anxiety and PTSD. It's going to take some time for her to come back to normal and many doctor visits to help her out of that trauma. I can take you to her some time this week if you like?"

"Yes please, I would love to see her and help her get well. Maybe I can take care of her so Matteo can go back to work and that will be my thing I do every day to keep busy."

"I think she would enjoy that and I think it's good for you, so you don't feel so alone here when I'm at work."

After we discussed everything we needed to, we both ended up sleeping until the next morning. I was a bit scared that after our talk, she would change her mind and go back to reality. I really want to be able to enjoy this phase of my life by sharing memorable moments with the person I call my partner. Olivia is everything I've been waiting for. I never knew she could be the one, I could have the chance to share my life with them one day get to call her my wife and the mother of my children.

CHAPTER 15

OLIVIA

After the shit show with Christian yesterday, I am glad the night ended on a better note with Luciano and I sleeping together in his bed. I wished he could've taken advantage of the heat of the moment we had after that passionate kiss we had but him being a gentleman said that he would like to take me on a proper date before he actually goes any further intimately. I can't believe this is my life. I know I shouldn't be thankful for what I am about to say but I am so happy I met Luciano the way I did because if I wouldn't have gotten kidnapped I wouldn't have met him. Everything happens for a reason and God wanted me to get over Christian with a man I deserve. I can tell he was raised by a good woman. Luciano's mother really did a great job with him. I wished I could have met her. The light was shining bright in the room waking us up. Luciano hugged me tighter when he felt me move. I started moving my ass back to him since I had my back to his chest. I wanted to tempt him a little and see if he had any self control.

"Baby girl if you keep moving your ass like that, you are going to make me lose all self control."

I laughed so hard because I knew that I could make him lose it all. I will wait for that special moment to be intimate with him because I also want to be sure that this is what I want. I don't want to make the wrong decision even though I know that he is actually perfect. I just have to learn how to live in his world because I will no longer be able to be on my own without having eyes on me 24/7.

"Don't worry I was just messing with you. I'm going to head over to my room to get my things ready. I need to shower and then I can meet you in the kitchen to eat breakfast together okay."

Caressing his cheek I turned to get up from the bed but he stopped me by kissing me. I can't get enough of his kisses. The way he tastes and smells drives my lady bits crazy. I am in disbelief that I am with this man. He is so handsome, tall, muscular and kind hearted. After he pulled away to look at me after that kiss, I leaned into his ear and told him I really like him then got up quickly leaving him in bed. Before I stepped out of the room, he kept his hazel eyes on me while his cheeks were heating up. With a big smile I got out to head into my room.

It must have been about an hour when I met Luciano in the kitchen for breakfast. He had already made coffee and a nice Italian breakfast. We ate breakfast silently but our gaze kept each other entertained.

"Are you ready to go?"

"Yes, let me just get my phone from the room."

"After we are done in the warehouse, I will take you to see Abigail."

"Yes! Thank you. I was waiting to see her, I didn't know you would take me so soon."

"Well you did ask and I just want to make sure I give you everything you want."

I walked to him, standing on my tippy toes. I hooked my arms behind his neck to kiss him. He grabbed me by the waist enjoying the kiss. We pulled apart then he took my hand in his leading me to the elevator to go to the parking lot. When we got to the warehouse, it was full of people. All of his workers will get to see the repercussions.

I was led into a big room where everyone was in a circle. I couldn't see the middle because everyone was taller than me. Luciano, still holding my hands, led me to the middle, as we got closer I was able to see Luigi kneeling on the floor with just his pants on and his hand tied up with chains pulling them up from the ceiling. Luciano told me to stand next to him so he could address everyone.

"Everyone listen up, we are gathered here because I called this meeting to show every single one of you what could happen if you decide to betray my family. Not everyone knows Luigi, he worked for us at the nightclub where my brother Ace is in charge. Luigi decided to take advantage of the opportunity my brother had given him by stealing money little by little until he no longer needed it. He bought his own warehouse about twenty minutes away from here. Matteo found out what Luigi had been doing. Luigi decided to make business with the Romanians by getting into trafficking women and children that come to tour Italy. I will not condone anyone overstepping my authority and trying to make business that we have deemed as inhumane. My brothers and I decided that we would not be doing human trafficking when my father passed the family business to me but then Luigi decided to go with it anyways, now he is going to face the consequences of betraying us and taking it upon himself of starting a business we most definitely didn't give permission. I also want to mention the last thing— This here is Olivia, she is one of the victims that I rescued from Luigi's warehouse. You all will respect her and look after her safety any time you see her around. Olivia is with me now. She is "Mine", no one will dare to defy my orders or look at her with lust because you will face the same consequences as Luigi."

Everyone kept looking around each other to see their reaction. Luciano asked everyone if they understood, they all agreed with him. Luciano whispered in my ear to head out to the car and wait for him there. He gave me a tiny peck on the lips letting everyone know I was his. I took a good look at Luigi before turning towards the exit. I was curious as to what Luciano had planned but I also didn't want to hear or see the aftermath. I wanted Luigi to pay for all the bad things he did to all of us and more because of the children that were already sold. After twenty minutes in the car, Luciano opened the driver door. I looked up from my phone seeing him looking hot as always. His clothes were still the same but he had a few drops of blood on his neck. I took some napkins from the middle console to clean him up. Thanking me, he turned to intertwine his fingers with mine.

"Are you ready to go see Abigail? Matteo is waiting for us."

"Yes I am— Lucky? Did you make it hurt?"

"You bet I did baby, you don't have to worry about him anymore. No one will hurt you ever again, not as long as you are with me. I will always protect you."

He drove to Matteo's house, we were mostly quiet on the drive. I can sense Luciano's unease. I'm not sure how many lives he's taken since his father entrusted the business to him. It must not be easy every time he has to do this. I know I would be shitting my pants if I had to kill someone. When we got to Matteo's house, Luciano opened the door for me, leading me up to the doors where we waited for Matteo to open up. Matteo opened the door after the second knock. He hugged Luciano and nodded his head towards me.

"Can I see Abigail please?"

"She is resting in the guest room but I know she will be content to see you here, please follow me."

He led me to the guest room, he left me inside on my own while him and Luciano mentioned that they would be talking about work in the office. I sat down next to Abigail grabbing her wounded hand. Tears started flowing because I couldn't believe what she had to endure many times to save me from them. She took the biggest hit, all to prevent them from taking me from doing the same things they did to her. I must have been sobbing loudly that I woke Abigail up.

"Hi— are you okay? Stupid question but I just want to know if you will ever be okay?"

"Don't cry Olivia, I will be fine. (Cough) I'm just trying to rest and recover from everything I went through. Please— (cough) don't worry about me."

“Are you catching a cold? Why do you keep coughing? Is Matteo giving you proper treatment here?”

“Matteo has been the sweetest, he has been taking care of me non-stop. He has called every doctor to try and fix me. I don’t have a cold, I just keep trying to catch my breath but I feel like I am out of it. Luigi’s man kicked me when I tried to fight them off. They bruised me inside making it hard to breathe.”

“I am so sorry Abigail, I should have fought harder so they wouldn’t hurt you more. I was a coward. I am sorry.”

“Shh— Olivia please I can’t see you crying like this. I did it because you remind me so much of my little sister and I couldn’t let them hurt you.”

“Luigi is dead! He can’t hurt us any more.”

“That is really great news, I am so glad he got what he deserved. I would’ve wished I’ve been there to see it unfold or even would’ve loved to have done it myself”

“No Abigail, don’t say that.”

“Olivia, don't look at me like that, I am not the monster. He was! He had his men RAPE me! I was raped so many times then I was hit also. It was horrible. I don’t know if I’ll ever be the same or if I’ll be able to have a normal relationship with a man because this has caused me to be in distress.”

“I am so sorry Abigail. I will be coming every other day to take care of you until you feel better and no longer need me. This is the least I could do to help you, for all the things you did for me. Please let me— please?”

“Thank you Olivia, It’s going to be so much better having you here keeping me company. That way also Matteo can get back to his life, he has been so busy with me, spoiling me with everything I need. I don’t want him to take time out of his day for me. I would rather have you here. Thank you.”

“You’re welcome.”

After I got done talking to Abigail, I went to the kitchen to get her more water. As I was walking back, I saw the office door slightly opened. I got close to it to hear what Matteo and Luciano were talking about. They were talking about what Luciano had done in the warehouse to Luigi. The way he was explaining it to Matteo was so gruesome, I decided to walk back to the room because I didn't want to hear about it anymore. I opened the door to the guest room finding Abigail having a seizure, I got so scared seeing her convulsing that I screamed to the top of my lungs. Luciano and Matteo both came in running with their guns out. Matteo reacted first, trying to tilt Abigail to her side. He took out his phone to dial someone. Not even five minutes went by, a man with a white coat came in. A doctor on call started working his magic on Abigail. He told us to wait outside while they calmed her down. Luciano took my hand pulling me out of there. As we got outside, I couldn't take it anymore. I started sobbing, I hated it seeing her like this. Luciano hugged me tightly letting me know he was there for me. In that moment I promised myself to never ever be a coward. Seeing my friend in this condition has made me realize that if I would have stood up for myself to Luigi maybe just maybe the damage done to her could've been less or spread out between us and she would've been able to recover just like how I did when I got out. Luciano set me in the car so he could drive me home, I was exhausted and all I needed was to be with him.

CHAPTER 16

LUCIANO "LUCKY"

The screams of Olivia are still stuck in my head, she scared me when she started screaming when Abigail started having a seizure. Matteo and I both pulled our guns out thinking the worse. After the doctor saw Abigail, I took Olivia home. I could see how distressed she was. I was needed at home by my father but I did not want to leave Olivia home by herself. On the drive I told Olivia I needed to make a pit stop but didn't really give her more information. When I got to the mansion, I could tell Olivia's expression changed. Of course anyone that comes here has the same expression. Our house was huge, we have acres and acres of land here. I pulled in front of the double doors, turning to her.

"This is my childhood home, I'm sorry I didn't tell you we were coming here. My father called me letting me know I was needed here. If you want you can stay here in the car or come with me inside."

"I'll come inside with you. Do you know how long it will take?"

"I don't think it will be long, you can get some food or something while I get done talking to my dad."

I went around the car to open the door then guided her to the double doors, I stopped before we went inside because I was a bit hesitant on what my father wanted to talk about. I proceeded to unlock the door, went inside and she grabbed my elbow gasping at how big this house is. As soon as we took another step, my father came out of the office yelling. I combed my hair with my fingers trying to calm down. Olivia looked at me nervously but I intertwined my fingers with hers to reassure her that I was here to protect her. My father stepped right in front of me, looked me in the eye then looked at Olivia.

"Dad, let me introduce you to Olivia—- Olivia this is my father Giuseppe Salvatore"

"Nice to meet you sir—"

"Is this why you have been too distracted at work? For a used girl? How come I just found out what you did today at the warehouse? Why didn't you mention anything?"

"Hey— I will not let you disrespect Olivia, if you want to be mad! Be mad at me! She has nothing to do with it, she was a victim."

"Figliolo, questa ragazza ti sta facendo prendere decisioni sbagliate. Lei stata usata, e ora vuoi quello che Luigi ha già avuto? Perché non hai raggiunto un accordo con Luigi e I rumeni, così avremmo potuto guadagnare di più denaro?"[1] ("Son, this girl is making you make bad decisions. She was used, and now you want what Luigi already had? Why didn't you reach an agreement with Luigi and the Romanians, so we could have earned more money?")*

"Andiamo in ufficio a parlor!" [2](Let's go to the office and talk!)*

I looked at Olivia, thanking that she does not understand Italian because I didn't want her to hear what my father just said. I whispered to her ear that I was going to the office with my father to talk. I told her where the kitchen was then she started moving towards that direction. When I came inside the office my dad was already sitting

---

1. "Son, this girl is making you make bad decisions. She was used, and now you want what Luigi already had? Why didn't you reach an agreement with Luigi and the Romanians, so we could have earned more money?"
2. Let's go to the office and talk!

down in his chair waiting for me to start talking. I told him everything that happened but he was still mad that I didn't make business with the Romanians.

"When you passed me the family business, I warned everyone about Human trafficking. My mother would be turning in her grave if she knew what you wanted me to do. I will not condone Human trafficking again in our organization. We can do weapons, drugs and money laundering but not that. We do not play with women and children's lives."

"Fine! You are being stupid son! But I will let you decide since you are now in charge."

"Is there anything else you want to talk about? I would like to leave already."

"Are you no longer staying in this house? I haven't seen you set foot here in weeks."

"It's time for me to be more independent, I've been living in my penthouse with Olivia. And don't dare to mess with her! I am happy with her, I will protect her at all cost if you dare to disrespect her!"

"Oh son! You do know that she is your weakness now! You better take good care of her because the moment she is alone, your enemies will try to hurt her to hurt you."

"I know— you don't need to tell me what I already know. I can take care of myself and her. Have a good night father."

"Abbi cura di te, ragazzo mio!" [3](Take care of yourself, my boy!)*

I stepped out of the office, all I wanted was to find Olivia and go home. Before going to the kitchen, I went to my brother's room. I went into Ace's room first, finding him laying down in bed on his phone.

"How's the nightclub?"

"Fuck Lucky! Don't you know how to knock?"

"I do, I just didn't want to."

"What if you would've found me jerking off fucker?"

---

3. Take care of yourself, my boy!

"Oh fuck! You're right! My bad."

"The nightclub is going well, I— I started doing the recounts of the numbers and receipts. Everything looks to be going— going well."

"Then why do you look so tense?"

"I just have been dealing through a lot with everything from what happened with Luigi but also my problems."

"You know you can talk to me right?"

*"Yeah, it's just that there's this girl that has been coming around the nightclub and I don't want any trouble. Her name is Aurora, she's stubborn, probably going to cause me trouble with her father Stefanno Bianchi who is the Chief Police that has been eyeing our organization for some time now, I am trying my hardest to make sure she doesn't get in any trouble at the nightclub to set her father off into looking into our business. Don't worry, okay, I'll deal with it." (Read more about Ace's story in book 2)**

"Okay, I trust that you will do what's right. I got to go, I'll be seeing you around."

I get out of the room to head into Chao's room. I was about to just go in without knocking but then I remembered what I just talked about with Ace and I decided to knock on his door but he did not answer. I sent him a text message to ask him where he was and he said he was still at school studying in the library. I start walking to the kitchen where I find my beautiful girl seated in one of the kitchen island stools, she was eating spaghetti that our chef had made for us.

"Are you ready to go beautiful?"

She got startled when I went inside the kitchen, and she almost choked on her food.

"Come and eat with me, there is no food at home. You haven't eaten since the morning, you need to eat."

"I just want to go home. How about I put some in a container to take home?"

"That works too, let's go home."

The chef got my food packaged then we got into the car to go back home. As soon as we got home, Olivia went to shower and I did the same. We both were going to meet in my room after we were done. I was done first, I wore shorts and no shirt. I laid on top of the bed waiting for her to come in. Olivia came into the room about fifteen minutes later with my packaged food. She said that I needed to eat it otherwise she would be going back to her room if I didn't eat. I ate then went to brush my teeth. When I came back to the room, I wasn't prepared for what I was seeing.

"Baby you are going to kill me in those shorts. What are you doing bending down like that?"

"Sorry I dropped my phone under the bed and I can't find it. Do you mind getting it for me?"

I don't know what she is trying to do to me, I'm trying to have self control around her but she is making it really difficult. I lowered myself down next to her to grab her phone but the phone was nowhere near the bed. When I stood back up she was in the middle of the bed being provocative. She tapped my chest with her toes, I grabbed her leg pulling her to the edge of the bed.

"What are you doing my beautiful?"

"Mm.. Nothing, did you find my phone?"

"No I didn't find it, you know it's not under the bed. Just tell me what you want, baby."

She looks towards the bed night table, following her gaze I find her phone charging behind the picture frame. I look back at her and she is smirking with a flirty look.

"I don't want to wait until you take me out on a proper date Luciano, I want you right here right now."

"Are you sure baby? All you have to do is just say the word. I will give you the world baby."

"Then take me now please."

I didn't stop myself this time because my baby wanted me. She wanted all of me and I wanted her too. I lowered myself to kiss her, she grabbed me by my neck pulling me closer to her. She hooked her legs on my waist feeling my hard-on. She kept on raising her hips, I started kissing her neck then back to her lips. She pulls away for a moment to tell me that she is so wet. I grab the hem of her shirt and pull it up leaving her in her bra. I take a good look at the most gorgeous tits I've seen. I bring my hands to cup her breast then she goes to touch the indent in my pants which is obviously the hard-on I have. Her touch makes me shiver, her hands on me make me lose control. She starts unzipping my pants but I stop her because I want to undress her first. I grab the hem of her pants and underwear to take them off. She is left in my bed just with her bra on.

"I am naked and you are still dressed. That's not fair. Let me take those off."

"I'm not wearing a shirt, I only have shorts on. But please be my guest."

She pulls my shorts off, leaving me in my boxers. My cock is itching to come out. I take her bra off leaving her bare. I am just amazed about her curves on her body, she is just so beautiful. I grabbed the condom from my night stand but she took it away from me telling me to allow her to do it for me. She pushed my boxers down releasing my cock free. She bites her lips making me proud of my size. My cock is not an average size, I was blessed with an eight inch cock. She rolls the condom on then lays on the bed naked waiting for me. I get on top of her grabbing her legs to hook them on my waist. I teased her entrance with my cock and I can already feel how wet she is.

"You are so wet for me Blondie."

"Mmh.. I can't wait any longer, Lucky. Please don't make me wait."

"I just don't want to hurt you. I don't have an average size dick, I need to go slow for you."

"No— I can take it. Just please—!"

There is no need for saliva since she is super wet. I push just the tip inside her, making her gasp. I asked her if she's okay, to which she nodded. I push another inch until I am completely inside of her. She is super tight but feels so good. I don't really know what she likes but I want to make her feel good. I will eventually learn all of the things she prefers in bed but right now I will show her what I do best. While I am thrusting inside her, I take my fingers rubbing her pussy in circular motion. She is moaning so loud and I know she is getting there. While I am fucking her, I take one of her nipples in my mouth at the same time I am playing with her other nipple with my finger. I am getting ready to burst but I want to come with her at the same time.

"Oh my— I—I'm almost there."

"I am too."

"I want it harder."

"What my lady wants, my lady gets."

CHAPTER 17

OLIVIA

When we got home from Luciano's parents' home, we both went to shower. Once we were done we both met back in his room where I took him the food that was packaged for him. I felt really bad that he had not eaten anything since we were busy the whole day. I didn't even ask what exactly happened earlier and I don't think he would have told me either because he already said this would be too much for me. Once he finished the food, he left to put the container back in the kitchen and brush his teeth afterwards. I had this big idea on how to seduce him but I don't know what he likes yet. I went with something simple. I hid my phone behind the picture frame he has of his mom, then I got on all fours to make it seem I am looking for my phone underneath the bed. When he came into the room, I knew I had him in the palm of my hands because I had worn tiny shorts and a tank top. Once he realized what I was doing he pulled me to the edge of the bed to ask me what I wanted. I like how he always wants to make me feel comfortable, wanted, and always listens to what I like. We started making out until I was naked then he was naked on top of me. One thing led to another, I never felt so loved in my life. Not even when I used to have sex with Christian. He never made me feel the way Luciano does. Luciano takes his time, learns and shows me how good it can be. When he pushed in the tip, I was already so wet for him. At the time when he took off his boxer and saw his length, I was speechless. He is huge, not even Christian that is six foot tall has Luciano's cock length. I wasn't complaining because after taking just the tip, he almost made me come immediately. It was that good.

"Harder! I wanted harder plea—-"

"Baby, get on all fours, I want to see that ass."

I got on all fours for him, he entered me once again sliding without difficulty. He grabbed my ponytail tugging it a little bit while he hit it from the back.

"Oh— my— God—"

"Does that feel good baby? I can feel you are almost there."

"Yes— ahh— I'm coming."

"I am too."

I felt the warmth of his cum inside me, making me extremely conscious that we used protection and I wish he hadn't. I don't even know why I am thinking of this but I could just imagine myself with my swollen belly carrying his child. I never really thought about kids with Christian, he made it impossible to talk about kids because of his demanding career. I always loved kids but never really thought about having them until now. I know I might sound delirious because I just met Luciano a couple of weeks ago but he's made me feel everything no one has ever made me feel.

"Wow, that's all I have to say."

"That was the best sex I've ever had"

"Really? How many people have you had sex with?"

"You are not seriously asking me this after we just had sex right.."

"I am, I want to know everything about you."

He didn't even hesitate when he said he had been with more

than twenty people. Even told me that his father paid someone to have sex with him. After he responded to my question, he didn't even ask me the same.

"Why didn't you ask me the same question?"

"Well.. Because your past is your past and I am fine with you having a past. I don't need to know your body count because all I know is that I will be your last because you are mine. You hear me MINE!"

When he shows me how possessive he can be, turns me on. I get that some people might think it's a problem but I enjoy it. It makes me feel wanted and that I belong to someone I lo—? *Wait? Was I going to say love? It's too fast right?*

After the amazing sex we just had, sleep came over us. The next couple of days went by fast which became a routine for us. Luciano would wake me up with his head between my legs then we would both shower. We would both eat breakfast then he takes me every day to Abigail's. I spend hours and hours on end with her. Making her company mostly because everyday she is starting to feel a little better. I take this opportunity to draw in my portfolio, which Abigail gives me lots of feedback. Matteo since then has gone back to work since I now stay with Abigail. The only time I see him is when I get to his house and then we leave because other than that I rarely see him anywhere else. Luciano has security for me, anywhere I go. I feel it's a bit much but I get it, he is trying to protect me from his enemies. I like to test him sometimes by rebelling in doing something I'm not supposed to because I love giving him a hard time, most times it ends up with him on top of me or I on top of him.

"Abigail come with me to the mall, I need new clothes and so do you."

"Olivia, I don't think we are supposed to go anywhere without protection. Since I've been here, I have learned Matteo's every move and he does not go anywhere without his weapon which must mean they are always at risk. We could also be and I don't want to be at risk with what just happened to us."

"I understand but we cannot keep living in fear. We need to go out and live a normal life without being scared of getting kidnapped again.

After I gave her my honest opinion, she seemed to have thought about it because she all of a sudden told me to grab my purse, that we were going shopping. The security guys that Matteo left in place were so busy eating lunch that they didn't even notice we grabbed a car from Matteo's garage. I am seriously hoping this little adventure gets to Luciano's ears so he can pin me against the wall, then put me over his knees to spank me to tell me how naughty I was by defying his words. I drove Matteo's car to the nearest mall. I had to use my phone's GPS to get around the city. We made a stop at a designer shop to look at this beautiful dress we saw from outside. The lady that worked there looked at us with a weird eye. She spoke to us in Italian but I didn't understand her. I spoke English to her then she responded back in English. She gave me bad vibes. I tried on the dress but the lady kept looking back at me from a distance. She got on the phone a minute later and took her attention from us. Abigail told me she understands Italian because she took classes in New York before coming here, which it's smart because if I would've learned it, I could've understood people who are always trying to talk to me in Italian. After some time later that I had tried on the dress, I told Abigail that I wanted to take it. Luciano had given me a card to be able to spend money until I could get my money back. I took the dress to the register where another girl assisted me with the purchase. As soon as I was putting the card back in my purse we heard people screaming. Abigail and I turned around to see what was happening. Abigail froze in place, I couldn't get her to move. The nice lady that assisted me locked the doors to make sure whoever was the cause for the screams couldn't come in. I was starting to panic. Then I saw two men in balaclavas coming in our direction. Abigail was still standing in the middle of the store, I had to pull her to the side to hide. The nice lady asked us if we were famous or celebrity. Then the lightbulb in my head turned on. Made me realize that maybe the other girl had called someone but how did she know we could be targeted or how did she know that I know Luciano. What gave it away? The only thing in my mind that kept taking me back was when we were in cages. I couldn't freeze just like Abigail, I had to do something. I grabbed my phone from my purse to call the only person I know will keep me safe.

"Hi baby, are you having fun with Abigail? I miss you."

"Lucky—?"

"Blondie is everything okay?"

"Please don't get mad but I took Abigail out to the mall. Everything was going great until we got spotted by someone. We are in a designer store inside the mall. There are two men with masks trying to get into the store but the lady that was helping us locked the door. Abigail is frozen in place, she is probably going into shock. Please—"

"Olivia— Olivia? Hello?"

Call dropped

Ring—Ring

"Baby I'm on my way"

Hangs up...

My phone got disconnected a couple of times after that. I think they either have a machine to block out the calls or something is not right with my phone. I don't even know how Luciano will be able to find us, I didn't even tell him my location. I decided to message him exactly where we are. Not even ten minutes later, I hear gun shots outside of the store. I am trying not to look but I want to know if the two men are shooting at the door in order to open it. After the gun shots, I hear someone knocking on the front door. The nice lady looks at us then says,

"Girls, do you know those people outside?"

I peaked a little bit to see Luciano and Matteo with their guns out knocking on the door to come in.

"Yes, that's my boyfriend!" *boyfriend? What the heck? He hasn't even asked me!*

The lady goes to the front to open the door. Luciano and Matteo get inside the store. The first thing Matteo did was to grab Abigail but since she was still in shock, he carried her out to the car covering her eyes so she couldn't see anything. I was still seated on the floor on the side of the register, when I looked up his Hazel eyes came into view. I gave him a smile but all I could see was anger pouring through his eyes. He pulled on my arm hard to take me back to the car. He was furious. I get that I put not only myself and Abigail in danger but he was being a bit too rough.

"Luciano, let me go! You are hurting me."

"We will talk about this at home."

I got inside the back of the car where Matteo and Abigail were already waiting. The whole ride I looked towards the window quietly. Everyone was quiet. I know I had said before that I wanted Luciano to know that I defied his words so we can have angry sex but I didn't think this was going to happen. Everything has gone wrong. Just when I was getting Abigail more comfortable to go out and stop being scared this shit happened. Matteo took us back to his place because he wanted Abigail to rest, he also mentioned about firing the security people he left in charge because they did not notify him about our leave. Once Matteo and Abigail were out of the car, I stayed in the back of the car quietly still. Luciano got into the driver's side and started driving us home. When we got there, I didn't wait for him to open my door. I got out and slammed his door. Thankfully he had given me a spare key. I took the elevator without him towards his penthouse. Once inside I went straight to my room, locked it without a thought and threw myself in the bed to cry. I was feeling all the emotions. I was feeling sad, mad, fear, and anger most of all. Luciano knocked on my door a couple of times but I needed space from him at the moment.

"Olivia, open the door!"

"NO!"

"Open the door or I will break this door down."

"GO AWAY!"

It didn't take him long, he grabbed I guess the spare key to this room to open the door. His angry face had already disappeared, he looked more at ease but still wanted to be with me. He erased the space we had by stepping in front of me. He pulled me to sit then hugged me so hard as if he needed to make sure I was still alive with him.

CHAPTER 18

LUCIANO "LUCKY"

After the best night of my life, we were able to fall asleep quickly. The next morning I was able to digest everything that happened yesterday regarding Luigi. I didn't want to go into details on how I went about things with Luigi's death. I am still not used to taking someone's life but this was necessary. I was not going to let someone step all over me and my family because then anyone can try to do that. I needed to show authority. After the shit show that happened at my father's house it simply was erased by the best night I've ever had. The best sex I could have had and it happened with Blondie— My Blondie. Weeks had gone by, Matteo and I were back to working normal while Olivia and Abigail spent their time together. When Matteo was back to work, I debriefed him with what had happened to Luigi giving him more details since I only gave him a short story back when I was at his house last time. After I slashed all of his limbs, we set his body on fire so there wouldn't be any questions from the cops just in case. Matteo and I were working on getting more shipments in, then exporting some to other organizations. Ace also had called me to let me know business was going great on his side. All of a sudden my phone starts ringing. My face lit up at the name showing on my screen.

"Hi baby, are you having fun with Abigail? I miss you."

*"Lucky—?" (*she rarely calls me Lucky? What's going?)

"Blondie is everything okay?"

"Please don't get mad but I took Abigail out to the mall. Everything was going great until we got spotted by someone. We are in a designer store inside the mall. There are two men with masks trying to get into the store but the lady that was helping us locked the door. Abigail is frozen still, she is probably going into shock. Please—"

"Olivia— Olivia? Hello?"

**Call dropped—*

**Ring—Ring— (* I call her once more then she answers)

"Baby I'm on my way"

Hangs up...

When I got there with Matteo, we didn't even park the car in its regular parking place; we just parked right in front of the stores. I haven't told Olivia but the phone I bought her had already a tracking device inside for me to be able to track her at all times. I sound paranoid but it's for the best. I don't want anything to happen to her. I've already lost the most beautiful person that I loved dearly, my mother and Olivia is my person now. I will do anything to protect her. I knew exactly where she was, I told Matteo to go in front and that I would cover his back. We saw the two masked men trying to get into the store. Matteo stepped right in front of them quietly putting the gun behind the guys back then pulled the trigger. The other one turned around but I was quicker, I pulled the trigger hitting him right in the head. They both dropped fast. Matteo pulled the guy's balaclava, noticing both of their tattoos. These guys are with the Russians. Our other enemies that we have to watch out for. They are big in the organization. We made sure to wear balaclavas as well to not be identified by cameras. After we saw the guys' faces, we headed straight for the store knocking on the door. The worker opened it for us. Matteo went straight for

Abigail, I stayed behind to make sure no one else came with the Russians. After Matteo took Abigail to the car, I went to Olivia. I was seeing red at the moment, there is no excuse on how I treated Olivia but I was so angry at her. How could she endanger her life this way when I had told her since the beginning what could happen if they saw her out without security. My enemies will use her to break me. I grabbed her by the arm to pull her off the floor where she was crouching.

"Luciano, let me go! You are hurting me."

"We will talk about this at home."

Once back home she went to her room locking herself inside. I started to feel guilty for the way I treated her, I decided to go talk to her but she was not opening her door. I grabbed the spare keys I had to open the door. Inside I saw her red puffy eyes, knowing I am the one to blame for her cry. I moved quickly towards her because I didn't want any more space between us. I caressed her face then hugged her so tightly that I might break a bone. I never thought how much she meant to me until today that I heard the concern in her voice over that phone call. I don't want to lose her ever. She is Mine!

"I'm sorry I pulled you roughly back at the store. I was really angry but it's no excuse for me to be an ass. Can you forgive me?"

"Luciano you cannot ever do that. I don't know what came over you but I have never had anyone be rough on me like that. It scared me but it also made me really mad at you."

"I know I'm so sorry baby. I didn't mean to be so rough. I was just in my head. I thought I was going to lose you to those guys. They were there to kill you, torture you to get back at me. You are the most important person in my life and people know that I'm with you now."

I hugged her a second time, then I pulled myself off her to tell her the reason why I wanted her to have security or always go out with me because I or my team will be the only ones to be able to take care of her if something like this ever happens again. I pulled her off the bed, carried her putting her legs on my waist then took her to our room because that is her room now. I laid her down on the bed, then started to kiss her everywhere.

"I'm going to show you the consequences of your actions. Are you ready to be spanked?"

She nodded without a word, she knew what was coming. I got her undressed, then started kissing every inch of her curvy body. I wanted to make her feel good first, I got on my knees then started to lick her inner thigh. I moved to the entrance of her pussy. She gasped when I got deep between her folds.

"Luciano, oh my god. That feels so good, don't stop,"

I kept going until she screamed my name, she came hard.

I smacked her ass, "Get on all fours". She listened without complaint. I positioned myself at her entrance, I smacked her ass again a little bit harder this time and she moaned. I love the little sounds she makes. I smacked her again.

"You understand what you did wrong today, right? You cannot do that again!"

"I didn't think this would be a problem. I thought we would be in and out of the store but someone called them and I am pretty sure it was the first girl that helped us at the store. I didn't want to make you mad. I just wanted to go out with my friend and have fun."

"Olivia you cannot go out without protection. I already told you, I have enemies and they want to see me break. I would give my life for you Olivia! I would do anything for you but I refuse to let you be on your own without protection. I don't want to lose you."

I don't know why I am getting so emotional telling her my feelings. I've never had this happen to me. She is the only girl in my life that has ever made me feel the way I do. I won't let her risk her life because of me. I rather keep her away from me, sacrifice my love to keep her safe.

"Luciano, I promise I won't go out again without protection but I cannot live like a prisoner. I need to be able to defend myself. I won't always be home just waiting for you to get home."

"Olivia, if I have to sacrifice my love in order for you to be free, then I'll do it. I'll send you back to New York. I would rather have you far away safe than be here but in danger. I won't have it."

"I don't want to go! I want to stay here with you. I promise I won't do something so reckless like what I did today. Please don't make me go."

"I don't want to let you go, I— *I love you*!" The word left my lips without thinking of the aftermath. I know we just met a couple of weeks ago but I really do love her. She is quiet for a moment but then she turns around cups my face with her hands to kiss me passionately.

She whispers "I am so happy you said it, because I have been waiting to tell you I love you too."

"I really do love you, you are it for me. I wanted to tell you this since the day after you came back to me when I dropped you off at school. I know we had just met back then but I never felt like this for anyone else."

"Me either, I knew I loved you the day I slapped you for sleeping with me but you actually eased my nightmares away. Then we started spending our time together, I would miss you every minute we were apart. I didn't want to believe it but I had fallen for you hard."

I didn't want any more words to show her how much I love her, I wanted to show her with actions. We started making out with so much passion. I kissed her neck, bit softly by her earlobe, then kissed her stomach, her inner thigh then her breast. Everything about this moment was going to stay engrained in my memory.

"You have made me feel good tonight, let me take care of you now."

She got up from the bed, pushed me to lay down on the bed then she took my cock in her mouth. This was the first time she has ever done that. Not because she didn't want to but because I kept delaying it. She needs to adjust to my length, I didn't want to hurt her. She is taking me deep in her mouth.

"Oh baby, that feels amazing."

She moans, making my dick vibrate in her mouth. I pulled her off because I don't want to cum inside her mouth. I grab her to pull her on top of me.

"Ride me, use me to your pleasure baby."

She gets on top of me then lowers herself to push my cock inside her. Once in, she starts riding me. It feels so good.

"You are so wet and so tight baby."

She starts to go faster making me groan because the feeling is out of this world. I know I am near and she is as well. She is squatting up and down my cock, I grab both sides of her ass cheeks to help her bounce then she is going faster.

"I am so close, baby."

"I am too."

Then without warning I explode my cum inside her making me realize that we forgot to use protection. She throws herself to the side of me to lay down next to me. She looks up at me and at this point I am fairly quiet because I don't know if I should mention it or not. I don't want to ruin this perfect moment. I build the courage to tell her but when I turn to her she is already sleeping. I get up to go to the bathroom to clean up. I grab a wash cloth to clean her up as well. Once she is clean I lay next to her until sleep takes over me.

CHAPTER 19

OLIVIA

Last night was the best night ever, Luciano told me he loves me and I told him I love him back. I don't want to hide my feelings anymore. I have never felt like this ever. These emotions are so strong even my heart can't take it. I know my dad is looking upon me happy that I found real love. When I woke up, I was already cleaned from last night. Luciano must have cleaned me. He is not in bed with me. I touch his side and it's cold. He must have woken up too early. I grab the shirt he left behind, then put it on without pants, panties or a bra. I woke towards the kitchen, no sight of him. I walk to the living room and he is not there either. I go into the office but the door is locked. Wondering where he could be, I went to the other side of the penthouse. There is a door that I have never opened before. I hear music behind the door, I go to open it slowly to find Luciano working out those muscles that I am obsessed with. He is sweaty showing off his abs, those tattoos in his whole body that drive me crazy.

(Knock, knock)

"Am I interrupting?"

"No— no come on in."

"I didn't wake you up with my loud music right?"

"No not at all, I was wondering how you keep up with all of these muscles." Tracing my hands into his abdomen and making it my point to turn him on.

"You don't know what you are asking for, Blondie, keep doing that and I'll be taking you out of this room in my arms to be buried inside you again."

"Please do—(gasp)"

He carries me, hooking my legs on his waist. He takes his shirt off me leaving me naked again. I can already feel the protruding boner he has. He takes me straight to the bathroom without putting me down. He enters the shower turning on the water, I screamed because the water is cold. The water starts getting warmer then he is lowering his shorts off him. He pushes his cock inside me making me feel the way he only makes me feel, full of him— complete! He starts thrusting while my legs are hooked underneath his arms making his muscles more enticing. He comes and then I come. He pulls out of me making me feel like I lost part of him, missing the feeling of being complete. He gently sets me down on the shower tiles, his mind seemingly lost in thought.

"Are you okay? Did I do something wrong?"

Bringing him back to earth, he says softly, "There is something that I wanted to tell you about what happened yesterday."

"Okay what's going on? You're scaring me."

"Yesterday when we had sex, we were very irresponsible because we forgot to use protection."

Fuck, that's right we did not use a condom! We were so lost in the heat of the moment that we didn't even remember to use a condom. No wonder he is quiet, he must be thinking about everything that comes after this.

"Don't worry too much about it. I was not in my fertile days. I have a normal cycle and I know when I am ovulating and when I am not. Yesterday wasn't one of those days. I don't think it's possible to get pregnant when you are not on your fertile days. We can use a condom next time or I could go to the pharmacy to take a Plan B, or I can just go to the doctor to get on birth control."

"Whatever you want to do I'm fine with. I just wanted to make sure everything was okay between us because of this little issue?"

"Yes, don't worry about it, my love."

"My love! I love that. Can you keep calling me that please?"

Chuckling, I nod to let him know that I will keep calling him that. We get cleaned up and dressed.

"What are we doing today? It's the weekend, do you have to be at work today?

"I have to be at the warehouse for about an hour or so to finalize a shipment, but why don't you get ready. I want to take you out to eat, or maybe to the nightclub we own or to the bar? Once I come back you can choose where we should go."

I give him another nod, he gives me a kiss on the lips then one in my forehead then heads out to the elevator. Once I'm alone, I do a little happy dance because I have never been this happy. Well I have but that was when my dad was alive. Now Luciano is the one who makes me the happiest. I go into my closet to see that Luciano has bought me some clothes, nice dresses and some outfits. He must have done this recently because I don't think I saw these a few days ago. I grab a mini skirt with a cute glittery blouse because I want to tell him to take me to the nightclub he owns. I haven't been to a nightclub in so long. A few hours later Luciano gets home to find me on the couch doing my toe nails.

"My lord! You look stunning baby."

"Thank you my love. I got super cute for you but also because I have decided where I want you to take me."

"Where does my lady want to go?"

"I want you to take me to your nightclub. I haven't danced in so long."

"Sounds good, let me shower quickly then we will be on our way."

Thirty minutes later Luciano comes out dressed with a button up shirt, black pants, and black elegant shoes. His wavy hair is still damp, he is also wearing a woodsy cologne that 's making my inner thighs clench. If we don't get out of here now, I will take him right here, right now. We head to the garage, Luciano opens the door for me then he gets into the driver side.

"I hope you don't mind but I invited my brother Chaos and his friend Luca."

"I don't mind, the more the merrier."

Once we get to the nightclub, I am in awe because this is the biggest nightclub I have ever seen. It has two entrances in the front which Luciano said that one is for the actual nightclub bar and the other is for a brothel. I was so curious to see the brothel but that could be another day. Today I want to let loose and dance all my worries away. Luciano parks the car then we start heading to the front where there is security. They let him pass of course because they know he is the owner. When we get inside, the club is packed. Luciano gets a table near the bar then tells me that he will be back because he is going to get us some drinks. I am alone at this point but I am observing the whole place. The music is great, the people are very welcoming and the place is a vibe. Luciano gets back with two shots, a margarita and a drink for himself.

"What did you order yourself?" I am raising my voice at this point since the music is loud.

"I got a Negroni, do you want to try?"

"Yeah, thank you."

The Negroni is not my cup of tea, it's too much. I grab my margarita, pleased with this cocktail because it's not too strong like the Negroni. Joey "Ace" comes to say hello to us at our table. I can tell that he is distracted because he is not paying attention to what Luciano is telling him and he notices also.

"What is going on with you? Are you okay? What is keeping you distracted?"

"Nothing I'll deal with it, just enjoy yourself and your lady. I'll be back." Joey says.

"What do you think is happening with him?"

"I don't know but I will find out sooner or later. I know my brother."

Luciano grabs my hand then pulls me to the dance floor. We start dancing, he is not so bad. I didn't think he could dance since when I met him I thought he was a grumpy person but I see another side of him. Something he hasn't shown to other people except for me. After the music ended we started to go back to the table where we met Chaos and Luca. We all say hi to each other, they both go to the bar to order drinks.

"Baby, I need to head to the restroom. I don't want to leave you alone but I need to go, I had too many drinks. Are you okay until I come back?"

"Yeah don't worry, your brother is probably coming soon so I won't be on my own."

Luciano starts to head into the direction of the bathrooms while I am on my phone back at the tables. I am so focused on my phone that I don't see that to my left Christian and Anna are at a table drinking beer. I put my face down so they don't see me. I need to think what I can do, because I don't want them to recognize me then have them talk to me when I have no desire to talk to them. I quickly get up from my table to look where the bathrooms are. I head towards the direction Luciano went. I am walking towards a not so lit up hallway when I see Luciano against the wall and a woman really close to him talking into his ear. Jealousy consumes my entire being. She is too close to him and he isn't backing away. She grabs his hand and puts it around her waist, his face is still not showing any emotion but why isn't he telling her NO! I am starting to get upset. She then gets closer to his face like she tries to kiss him but he turns his face to my direction. That's when he sees me just standing there watching them. She smirks at me, so I decide to turn around and leave the nightclub. I ran outside to try and catch a taxi to go home. A taxi stops for me, I get inside leaving the place behind. All I see is Luciano coming out of the nightclub searching for me but he does not see me since I am already in the taxi. My phone starts ringing once, then twice. I lost count on how many times it rang but I never answered. I already know that it's Luciano that is calling but I do not want to talk to him. While in the taxi, my tears just start pouring out of me. I don't want to lose him but why didn't he do anything to stop her. Why did he let her get so close to him? Who was she? Was she an ex-girlfriend? I am so angry and sad because I wanted him to do something or tell her that he was taken but he didn't.

After some time I got home, I packed my bags and got out of his penthouse again. I took another taxi but this time I went to Matteo's house. I did not want to stay with Luciano.

"Olivia, what are you doing here? Is Luciano here with you?"

"No, we had an argument. Can I stay here for today? I'll leave tomorrow, please I don't have anywhere else to go."

"Yeah— yeah you can stay here. Does he know you are here?"

"I don't really care if he does or not. I am not talking to him right now."

Matteo let me stay in the guest room, he even brought me food before going to bed. In the room, I turned the phone back on to find many messages and missed calls from him. I opened the internet to check for flights going to New York. I see one leaving tomorrow morning. I know I am being childish for not letting him explain himself but I really don't want an explanation at the moment. I want to cool off and the only way I do things is by running away. I never told him that my passport was delivered recently so I am able to leave whenever I want. I use the credit card he gave me to buy the ticket. I leave a note for Matteo for him to find where I have placed a letter for Luciano, the credit card, the keys to his penthouse and the phone he bought me. I cried myself to sleep, then the next morning I tip-toed myself out of there to catch a taxi to the airport. An hour later, I am boarding my flight to New York without really thinking about anything because I just want to run away. I will deal with my feelings later.

CHAPTER 20

LUCIANO "LUCKY"

I tell Olivia that I am going to take her anywhere she wants, she decides she wants to go to my nightclub. When I got home from the warehouse, I found her looking stunning in that mini skirt she has on with a cute sparkly blouse. We head to the nightclub, where we enjoy drinks after drinks. We dance a bit, even though I am not a dancer. I wanted to make her dance because I didn't want to see her dance with no one else. After what seemed like a lot of drinks, I tell Olivia that I am going to the restroom. I didn't want to leave her alone but she reassured me that she would be fine since Chaos was coming back from the bar. I head to the back of the building where the restrooms are tucked in, in a low lit hallway. I go in, do my business but as I was coming out of the restroom I see someone I met many years ago and she is waiting for me.

"Serafina what are you doing here?"

"Nothing, I saw you come in with a really nice American girl. Who is she? Have you replaced me already?"

"There is no replacement because you and I were never a thing remember—"

"Bullshit, I told you I wanted something with you and you

denied me saying that you were too busy taking over your family business. Look at you now! By the hand of a gorgeous girl that isn't me."

"Serafina, what we had was never serious. I was always firm with you and told you what we had was nothing more than just sex."

"Oh yeah I remember, that's been the thing since we met. Do you remember how we met? Remember the day you took me to the back of the bar to fuck me then gave me money because you thought I was a prostitute? Then after a few days we saw each other again and we fucked again and again for months. Not only did I let you know of my feelings but you denied me so many times but I was hopeful. Now I am not because you are with someone else that is filling my shoes."

"Serafina— please stop, " I told you how I felt. I only needed a distraction for what I was going through with my family. I know it sounds fucked up but I was always truthful to you about my feelings. I told you that whatever we had was purely for sex and you agreed."

"I know, I know but a girl can dream. Please just give me another chance?" She tries to kiss me but I turn my face the other way. That's when I see my beautiful blue eyed girl just staring at us. Serafina followed my gaze because she smirked at Olivia. Not even a minute later, Olivia is running towards the exit. Fuck! I fucked up! I should've been more firm with Serafina and not let her get too close to me, but I panicked and didn't even move. I quickly pushed away from Serafina's hold to follow Olivia to the exit. When I get outside she is no longer there. She must have taken a taxi to the house. I try calling her phone and sending her messages but they all go unanswered. I try to track her phone but she must have turned it off because there is no signal. I get a notification on my phone about motion caught on camera. I open my camera app to see her going into her room. I go back inside to let my brother know I am going back home, that I will talk to him about what's going on with him later. About an hour later, I got home because traffic was brutal. Once inside I don't see Olivia anywhere in the house. I go back to my camera app to see what she has been doing the past hour. I found that she packed a bag then left the penthouse. I cannot track her because her phone is still off. Now I am getting worried because it's night time. Where could she have gone at this time? She knows she is not allowed to be on her own. I am pacing the living room when I get a message from Matteo.

> "Don't worry about Olivia, she is here with me. She asked me to stay the night. She told me to tell you to just let her be for tonight. You can come tomorrow to pick her up. Night bro."

I feel more at ease knowing she didn't go to a hotel or somewhere worse. She is safe at Matteo's house. I will give her the space she needs for tonight. But tomorrow morning I am going early to pick her up and then I'll explain everything she saw back at the nightclub. I go into my room feeling the emptiness of the house without her. I try to sleep but I just can't. I stayed up all night tossing and turning. As soon as the clock hits six in the morning, I am in my car heading to see her. It took me about two hours to get there because I had to stop by the warehouse about some issue my workers were having. By the time I get to Matteo's house it is about 8:30 am. I knock on his door, he then opens the door but his face expression is not something I see very often.

"Who died? Why is your face like that?"

"I'm sorry Lucky, I don't know where Olivia is—"

"What the fuck do you mean you don't know where she is. You messaged me yesterday that she was here and to not worry."

"I did but she must have left early in the morning. She did leave a note. Here—"

He hands me the note she left along with the spare keys, her phone and the credit card I gave her. I open the letter and I instantly freeze and go numb.

"Luciano, I am sorry to leave you without properly thanking you for all you have done for me. I know, you must see me as a childish woman for leaving without letting you give me an explanation. I am just tired of everyone I love, betraying my trust. Christian did it, my best friend Anna did, my own mother did, and now you! When I saw you with that beautiful red head girl I became instantly jealous. I couldn't contain it. She must have been a part of your life for her to be that close to you and for you to not be able to back away from her. All I want for you is to be happy and if it's with this girl then so be it. I am running away again, like I always do. This is the only thing I know how to do right in my life. Don't look for me please, I will call you soon whenever I feel like I am ready, then I will ask you to give me your explanation. For now I think it's best for me to part ways, be on my own and see where it takes me. I will always love you and have you deeply in my heart. I will miss you dearly Luciano. Have a lovely life."

- Your Blondie (Olivia)

Reading this letter, all of my happiness has left my body because without Olivia, I don't think I can be happy. I don't want her to go, I want her to listen to what I have to say, to let me explain that Serafina is in the past, that Olivia is my present and my future. I came to realize that I don't know where she lives in New York. I don't even have her number or how to find her over there. I leave Matteo, get in my car to start driving to the airport. I'm hoping to find her still there so I can explain. I make a call to Matteo while in the car and he already has the answer for me before I even ask the question.

"She bought a ticket to Manhattan, New York for nine in the morning."

"Thank you." I look at the clock and it says 8:40am, I am about ten minutes away from the airport. I accelerate the car going faster so I can make it before the time she boards the plane. As soon as I got there, I double parked not caring for my precious car. I speed through the crowd jumping the security points because I don't care to be taken to jail at this point if she is no longer going to be with me. I don't care about anything, I just want her. I get to the gate where the screen says her plane is boarding at this very moment, I run before the lady can close the door. She asks me for my boarding ticket but I ignore her. She grabs the phone to call on security but I am already inside. I go row by row until I see her in one of the window seats with her red puffy blue eyes. She has been crying and it's all my fault. I'm such a fucking asshole, why didn't I shoved Serafina away from me and made it known that I was taken. As soon as she sees me, her face shows confusion.

I kneel in front of her row seat where two other people are seating,

"Baby, please don't go. Let me explain to you everything." I am feeling so emotional which is unlike me, containing shedding tears because my father taught us to never cry in front of people because it's a weakness.

"What are you doing here Luciano?"

"Signore! Deve andare, la sicurezza sta già arrivando.[1]" *(Sir! You have to go, security is already on its way.) The flight attendant says.

"Luciano please, you're going to get in trouble. Just let me leave."

"NO! I don't want to ever let you go. You are MINE! You belong to me. I love you, I don't know what I'm going to do without you."

The flight attendant interrupts again but this time in English,

1. Sir! You have to go, security is already on its way.

"Miss, if you care for this man please have him get off this plane or accompany him out so we can get these people to their destination. If he does not leave, he will end up in jail."

I think the flight attendant got to Olivia because she is already standing up, grabbing her suitcase from the overhead compartment.

"Come on! Luciano get up!"

I get up slowly but I am still standing there without making a move. She sees that I am not leaving, she goes to grab my hand then looks me in the eye and says take me home. That one word makes my foot move instantly because she wants me to take her HOME. We make an exit out of the plane where two security guards are waiting for me. I pay them off so they can let me walk out of here with my girl. When we get to the outside my car is nowhere in sight.

"Fuck, I think they took my car."

"Who"

"To the impound, since I was double parked in a loading zone."

"You double parked that car you said it's your baby?"

"For you, I would do anything. I don't care that they took my car. I would do it again, If it brought me here to you."

I grab a cab letting him know where to take us. I'll have one of my men get my car off the impound. The car ride is awkward and silent. The mood has changed between us and I need to break out of it because we have never been awkward with each other. I also want to wait until we get home to talk because I don't want people knowing my business. When we get home, she sits down on the couch and starts crying. I can't take seeing her cry knowing it's because of me.

Cupping her face, "Please baby, please don't cry. I can't stand it when you cry because I know it's my fault,"

"Luciano, I'm crying because I didn't want to go but I always look for an excuse to run away. I know you are not at fault for anything except for not telling that red head to back away because she was too close to my man."

"I'm so sorry baby, please forgive me. I know I should've put a stop to her when she came too close. I had told her how I felt about her, which was that I had no feelings towards her. She insisted and came on to me. I do not have feelings for her. I only have eyes for you."

"I'm sorry, I left so abruptly without thinking about anything other than myself. I just wanted to run away from a situation that had me doubting if I was enough for you. I wasn't enough for Christian and maybe I thought—"

"Don't! Don't ever say that baby. You are more than enough for me. You are my world. You complete me."

I couldn't contain myself any longer, I carried her into the room because I was about to show her with actions how she is enough for me.

CHAPTER 21

OLIVIA

Inside the plane I am the most devastated I have ever been. I'm in a window seat waiting for everyone to board the plane. I look up to see those hazel eyes I love. He is here! How did he get inside? He kneels in front of my row to tell me not to go. He tells me to let him explain and to please forgive him. I already know I am going to give in because I can't stand to see him hurt. The flight attendant says something to him in Italian that I couldn't understand but then she looks at me to tell me in English basically if I don't want to see Luciano go to jail to get him out of here. Knowing that if he goes to jail he could end up there for other things I decide to get up, get my suitcase then head out. He is still standing there as if he still needs to explain himself. I don't want him to explain himself at this moment. All I want is to go home. I tug on his hand, pull him out of there, "Take me home". I can't believe he got his precious car impounded for me. We arrived home, we talked and cried, well mostly me. After he explained himself and I did also, he couldn't resist taking me in the room. He carries me into the room, lays me down, undresses me then starts kissing me as if it's the last time. That night he made love to me. He didn't just make love, he showed me how to feel loved. He showed me how good it is to be with him. He pleasured me and I pleased him, which was something I wanted to do since we got home but we needed to talk and explain to each other what happened back there. I reacted like a total teenager. He of course given his age did not. He was mature about the situation. I need to work on some things about myself and not run at the first issue we have. The next day, I woke up to the smell of coffee. Luciano is no longer in our bed. I get up, head to the bathroom to fix myself a little, then enter the kitchen to find him drinking his coffee and reading something on his phone.

"Morning"

"Morning baby, how did you sleep?"

"Delightful since I was next to you of course."

"I have to go to work, will you be okay staying home on your own until I come back?"

"Actually I was thinking of going to Palermo University. I want to see if they have any other classes I can take in the meantime."

" That sounds perfect, I'll have Giani or Alonso accompany you to school. I don't want any complaints about them being with you all day while you are out because you know it's not safe being alone."

"I know— I know. Can they stay outside of the classrooms though? I don't want people questioning me."

"Okay I'll let them know to stay outside. Have a nice day baby."

He kisses my lips then my forehead like he always does then he is out of there. I make a mental note to get used to having security with me at all times. I sigh because I really don't want to cause attraction or distraction. I shower, get dressed. By the time I am ready Giani is waiting for me in the lobby. He takes me to Palermo University, I talk to a counselor about the program I was supposed to be in and the event that transpired and caused me not to go in the first place. The counselor gets in contact with my Professor Dean which explains how good of a student I am. The counselor is impressed with my grades and all of the hard work I have done.

"Olivia Wilder, I think I can work something out with the professors here that are in charge of the program to reinstate you so you can finish the program in about 4-5 months with a degree but you have to work extremely hard. Do you think you can do that?"

"Oh my gosh, YES! I CAN! I will work double if I have to, I just need this opportunity to get started on my career. Thank you so much. You won't regret it."

I get out of there with a smile from cheek to cheek because I know it will be completely challenging to do but I know I can do this. It will give me something to do instead of being at home all day, and it will be the start of my career. I can't wait to tell Luciano. Once back home I get started on dinner. I cooked Alfredo pasta, I know it's not the traditional Italian pasta but whatever I cook is always delicious. My dad used to love being in the kitchen and he showed me a few things here and there. My mother never cooked so my father always took the initiative to make something so I could eat. After I got done cooking, I showered then waited for Luciano to get home. About an hour later, he sent me a message saying he would be home late to not wait up. I pre-packaged all the food into containers then went to sleep. I was a bit upset that I was going to need to wait until the next day to tell him the good news. As soon as I went to bed, I fell asleep. I must have been really tired because I didn't even wake up when Luciano got home. As I am tossing in bed to touch Luciano, I feel nothing. I touch the side where he sleeps on, it's cold and the bedding is still intact. I look at the time which points to eight in the morning. I don't smell the coffee he always does in the morning and now I am getting worried. I ran to the kitchen, he wasn't there. Living room no signs of him. I am walking to the gym area because he loves to spend time there but the lights are off and there is no music playing. Weird!... I walk back to see if by any chance he is in the office but the door is closed and locked. I knock just in case but no one answers. I need to call him to see where he is. As I am walking back to the room to get my phone, I hear the door unlock.

"Sorry Baby, I've been so busy that I completely forgot to send you a message that I was going to stay at the warehouse."

His facial expression is different, there is something he is not telling me. I have gotten to know him pretty well in these few months. There is something bothering him and he doesn't want me to worry.

"Luciano, I was so worried when I woke up and didn't find you at home. What happened at work? And tell me the truth please. I could see in your eyes that something is worrying you."

"I didn't want to worry you but I think it's best you know that by being with me you are always in danger. I stayed at the warehouse because I was just briefed that the Russians have taken a step further into getting revenge on the two people we killed outside the store but also about Luigi's death. His family have teamed up with them to get revenge. They sent me a note saying eye for an eye coming soon. Which means they will be coming for the people I love starting with you."

"What can we do? Now that we have a heads up about their possible threat against me."

"Olivia is not a possible threat, it's a threat already in the works, like a ticking bomb just waiting to happen. You know what this means right?"

"No, what does this mean?"

"No going out at all. You are to stay inside at all times. I cannot protect you on my own if you are outside of these walls. I need to prepare my people to fight but I am not also risking anyone's life."

"NO! No— I can't Luciano, I can't!"

"What do you mean you can't! I am not fighting with you about this. You are to stay here and that's it. I will lock you if I have to."

"NO!NO! Luciano, yesterday that I went to the university they offered me to join the program again for my designing career and I was told that I have to work really hard because I have to be ready in 4-5 months to graduate. I cannot stay locked up here, I need to go out and do this program! This is why I came here to Italy in the first place."

"I'm sorry but you are not going to do the program. I am not risking your life for a silly program that I can pay for you to do at home."

"Excuse me! Silly? This is my life and I want to do the program. You don't get to dictate my life because we are together. You can put full security on me if you have to but I am doing this program."

"Olivia! Don't make me regret this..."

"What do you mean?"

"I am buying you another ticket to fly home. Until things get better over here, I need you to go to New York. I will bring you back once I have dealt with the Russians."

"You can't do that! You wouldn't... You just stopped me from leaving yesterday, you cannot send me back."

"Yes, I can! I will tie you down if I have to but I am taking you to the airport and sending you back to New York."

"If you send me back to New York, don't bother coming back for me! This will be over! You hear me!"

I leave the living room without looking back at Luciano because I feel betrayed. I don't want to go. I know I was ready to leave yesterday because I was being childish but now that I know that I am able to finish the program and I love Luciano, I do not want to go! He knocks on my door but I am too angry to reason with him.

"Olivia, open the door please. We have to talk about this."

"NO!"

"Do you want me to use the spare keys again? Just open it."

I get up to open it, all I see in his hazel eyes is fear. Fear of losing me, Fear of having to deal with loss again. Fear of seeing me being used by the Russians because they want revenge. I don't want to see him eye to eye because I know that I will give in to his request but then that means I lose the chance again of being in the abroad program for my career. He grabs my hands to get my attention.

"I just called the counselor at your school, I told them that there is an emergency in New York that you have to attend to and they said that the professor will send you all work through the school email but you have to be back for the exam which is in about a month or so.

I think we can make that happen. Please let me send you back to New York, with all the pain in my heart I have to send you back to protect you. Let me deal with them, you can be back in four weeks."

"Fine, I really don't want to do this but I will go to stay safe. I don't want to leave you but if you are telling me to go to keep me safe I'll accept it."

Sobbing, he hugs me. Kisses my lips then my forehead like he always does then moves on to grabbing my suitcase from the closet to start packing some of my clothes, not all which gives me hope that he still wants me back. I don't have a good feeling about this but I will do anything for him to know that I am safe. He doesn't need to mourn another person he loves. We get to the airport, he kisses me again then I walk to the boarding gate to get into the plane. At this point we are both shedding tears because we do not want this but has to happen. The flight is about thirteen hours with one stop to Rome. I spent the whole flight sleeping because I am more tired than normal. When I get to JFK airport, I take a taxi to Manhattan which takes roughly about an hour with some traffic. I get home but since I don't have any of my keys, I knock on the door but then a neighbor comes out to let me know my mother has gone on vacation. I remove the potted plant we have outside to find spare keys which I always leave there for occasions like this. I get inside, go to my room, tossed myself in the bed to cry myself to sleep.

CHAPTER 22

LUCIANO "LUCKY"

After a night of showing Olivia how much she means to me, I had to go back to reality the next day. Back to work I went, leaving her to do her own thing. She said she was going to the university to talk to a counselor so I had Giani accompany her. After what seemed like hours, Matteo came into the office and his facial expression showed that something had happened. The first thing I thought about was Olivia but he then handed me a note that he said was left outside taped to our door. When they went back to the cameras to see who it was, they saw a masked person delivering the note.

"Lucky, Lucky! You fucked with the wrong people. Those two people you killed recently outside a store were my people but also family. I didn't think you were capable of killing so many people. First was Luigi then my guys, well guess what! Luigi's family wants blood, I want blood, we all want blood. What a better way to get blood than eye for an eye. Take care of the little lady of yours because the moment she is on her own, I will have my men use her, use her again and again for their satisfaction, then I will dispose of her right in front of your house the same way you saw your mother all those years ago. You have been warned!"

Fuck, I can't let nothing happen to Olivia because of me. I need to get Matteo on this before it goes too far.

"Matteo, can you find out exactly who those guys we killed were? I know they were with the Russians but with what family. I need to know before we strike."

"I'm already one step ahead. I will be back in an hour with some answers. You should go home and talk to Olivia."

"I can't, she'll see right through me. I can't hide anything from her but I don't want her to know about this until I am certain about this threat."

"Okay, Lucky I hope you are doing the right thing."

Matteo leaves me in the office while I am trying to decide what to do. I sent Olivia a text message to not wait up , that I'll be home late. As I sent the message, I opened the camera to see her reaction and it's killing me to see her like this. She spent all evening cooking for me and probably wants to let me know about her day but I can't stop thinking about that threat and I don't want to ruin her day today. Hours go by, still waiting for Matteo to come back. I decide to stay here at the warehouse and face the consequences tomorrow. I know Olivia is safe at home and I have the cameras on to let me know of any movement. Matteo comes into the office hours later to let me know that the threat is very much real and that the Russian family that sent that, are one of the biggest in Moscow. I really fucked up by killing those two but also Luigi because they want revenge and they won't stop until they have Olivia. Knowing that she is my weakness they will break her to break me. I need to think fast about my options. The sun was rising, I must have fallen asleep at my desk. The time is showing at eight in the morning, I get in the car to drive home hoping that Olivia is not mad that I didn't show up to sleep. As I am getting inside, I find her walking towards our room but she stopped when I opened the door. She saw my worried face, most definitely had to talk about everything going on. I gave her the options we have. She makes it hard because she wants to stay here to finish her program but I keep telling her that I am not willing to risk her life. She gets mad then storms off into her room. I decided to call her school and bribe the professor with some money to let her do her school work online for at least a months. The professor agrees, and I send the transfer to their account. I head to her room to reiterate that she must leave or stay home at all times. She sees the worry in my eyes. I hate that we are even at this point because I don't want her to leave but If she goes back to New York, she is far away from the people wanting to attack her. She will be safe over there maybe until I deal with the situation here. She agrees to go, so I take her to the airport. I kiss her then her forehead, I do not want to let her go but it's for the best. She goes in since they are boarding the plane. Once the plane has left, I head to the warehouse to deal with this situation because I promised Olivia I will have this handled in a month, so she is able to be back for her exam at school. Matteo and I started planning how to hit them from every angle. I call my people and my brothers to join which they are happy to help. We spend days planning and planning to succeed but then I get another note. The Russians have been pretty quiet since Olivia left, I am not sure why send another note.

"Lucky, did you think that sending your girl far away would

work? We are ten steps ahead of you. If we can't get to your girl, we will get someone you love dearly here. Be prepared because we will hit when you least expect it."

Fuck, they know that I sent Olivia away but I am hoping they are dumb enough not to find out where. I need to let my brothers, my father and my people watch their backs just in case they strike soon. Matteo comes inside the office where I have not left since Olivia left for New York, I can't be at home because she is not there. I can't stand being in the penthouse without her.

"Lucky, I am getting Abigail to a safe house just in case they decide to look into the death of their people, they will find out that I was the one who killed the other guy."

"You really like Abigail huh?"

"Yeah I really do, I never thought I would like to settle down or have a family of my own in my line of work but Abigail has made me look at the world differently. Since I met her, she took my heart with her. She just doesn't know it yet but I am planning to ask her out on a date. Even though she has been living with me and getting better with her therapist, I don't want her to see me as someone to just be thankful for since I helped her. I want her to see me for me."

"She will, she is a really nice person from what I have talked to Olivia. I am happy for you."

"Thank you Lucky. I will take Abigail to the safe house tonight and take some of the guys with me to watch my back."

"Don't worry, take all you need."

Matteo leaves with Giani, Alonzo, Bruno and Carlo. It's been a two weeks since Olivia left, I haven't been in contact with her just in case they are tracing the information and somehow give out her location. What I didn't say to Olivia was that I was sending one of my men to watch her every move. Romeo is in New York watching her from afar to report back every night. I know she has been staying home, her mom is on vacation which means she is alone at home.

She has only come out twice during the week to drink a matcha drink, whatever that is. We are getting super close to having everything prepared for our strike, I just need to go over some things with Matteo before we actually execute it. My phone starts ringing but I silence it because I need to focus but then my phone starts ringing again. I pull my phone from my pockets to see who's calling. Romeo's name appears on the screen. I know he is going to report back but it's a bit early, he usually calls later. I answer the phone eager to know how Blondie is doing.

"Romeo, how's everything going?"

"Boss— Boss."

"Hello, can you hear me? I can barely hear you. Is everything okay?'

"No boss— Olivia had an accident."

The color of my skin went pale after that sentence. What does he mean she had an accident? How?

"What are you saying? What do you mean she had an accident? How? Romeo!"

"She had gotten out of the house, she drove her car so I followed two cars behind her. Out of nowhere a black car went head on to her car as if it was waiting for her. The car rolled two times then the black car disappeared. The ambulance is here now, they are taking her to the hospital. I think you should be here boss."

"Fuck! They made their move. They knew Olivia was sent away from here but I didn't think they would follow her all the way to New York. How is she? Do you know anything? Fuck! I should've been there with her. I should've never sent her over there to be on her own."

"Boss, they do not want to tell me anything because I am not family. Should I find out her mother's number to call her?"

"No, I'll be there later. I am taking the jet. Do not move from there. Keep your phone on."

I hung up the phone, started moving towards the exit then Matteo was about to leave with the guys but I stopped him to tell him what happened. He tells me that he will have the jet ready and to take half of the guys with me. I go to the penthouse to grab a few things then head out again to the location of the jet. Once I get there, I see half of my men standing outside waiting for me. We board the jet, the pilot lets us know that we will be there in about 10-13 hours. I am praying and hoping nothing happens. I need to get there fast but 10-13 hours is a long time to wait. I try to catch up on some sleep but I can't close my eyes. Every time I close my eyes I picture Olivia in that car just rolling. I picture her all wounded and not being able to talk to me. I try to take that picture out of my head but it's impossible. I get served alcohol hoping it would ease the tension I have. After hours of being in the jet, we got to JFK. I had Matteo rent a car for us to move around. I don't know how long we are staying but just in case we need to be able to drive to the hospital. We get inside the car, I drive because I don't want to blame anyone for taking longer than we are supposed to. The GPS is telling me that I will get to the hospital in about forty-five minutes. It's frustrating because I want to be there already. Romeo has not messaged me anything which means that he is still not getting any answers. When I get to the hospital, I double park at the emergency room entrance. I turned to my guys to tell them to take the car to the parking lot then to meet me inside. As soon as I am out of the car, I run to the lobby. I find a lady in the front desk, I ask her to point me in the right direction. I go up to the second floor, asking around if they have Olivia Wilder in one of the rooms. Then a nurse tells me that they do have her but they are only letting family in to see patients. Without a thought I tell her that I am her husband! She looks at me confused then tells me that her medical history shows her marital status as single. I told her that we got married recently in Italy, she seemed to believe that crap. She tells me to wait at the reception desk and that she will call the doctor. The doctor comes out heading straight to me.

"Hello, my name is Doctor Dupree. I am the head doctor in charge of Ms.Wilder. And you are?"

“Hi, My name is Luciano Salvatore, I’m Olivia’s husband. How is she?”

“Mr. Salvatore, Olivia suffered a concussion from the hit of the other car and her car rolling. She has a bit of swelling but nothing too serious. We are keeping her in observation to make sure the swelling goes down. The baby and her are doing great at the moment, she is resting. I administered a low dose of medication given her situation. Would you like to see her?”

“Excuse me? What baby? What are you talking about?”

CHAPTER 23

OLIVIA

It's been two weeks of just staying inside these four walls. I don't feel like doing anything. I am sad and tired, really tired. I didn't even know I could nap so much. I never nap. I've been ordering food to be delivered because I lack the motivation to cook anything myself. Then yesterday, I promised to not order anymore junk food because whatever I had ordered made me have an upset stomach, I threw up and couldn't stand the smell of it. I went back to sleep after that fiasco. An hour later I had the weirdest dream that made me wake up trembling because it felt so real. I tried going back to sleep but all I kept in my mind was Luciano's face. I don't know at what point I started thinking of all the things that have been happening then immediately I got up from bed to look at my calendar. Went to my night stand, grabbed my phone then opened the app I have to track my period. When I open the app, in big letters it reads "Period is late". I started panicking because I told Luciano that when we had sex I was not on my fertile days. Did I mess this up? I don't have any pregnancy test at home because I was on the pill with Christian and we were taking care of ourselves with condoms. I can't go to any store right now because it's late. I will need to wait until the morning to get some. I go back to sleep caressing my lower stomach because I am pretty sure I am pregnant. I'm never late, my periods have always been regular and precise on the dates. The next morning, I woke up nauseous.

"Thanks! Little one, now you want to make yourself known."

I decided to go get some decaf coffee since I know I can't take caffeine when pregnant. I get in my car to head to the nearest coffee shop before going to the pharmacy to get some pregnancy tests. Within five minutes of my drive, a car hits my car making my car roll. I lost all consciousness at this point. Everything is dark, I hear people yelling then I hear the ambulance but my eyes are still closed. All I want is for my baby to survive. I want this baby to live and thrive, I want to be able to surprise Luciano with this but I don't even know if I am going to make it. I must have been going in and out after the accident because I saw the medics taking me into the ambulance but then I lost consciousness again. It must have been hours after the accident, when I woke up I was at the hospital hooked up with a bunch of things in my arm, my nose, and my finger. As soon as my eyes opened, they felt heavy. My body felt sore and bruised when I tried to move everything was sore. The Doctor came into the room quietly lowering the light because he knew that it was bothering me.

"Hello, I am doctor Dupree and I am the one who is in charge of you for the moment. Can you tell me what you remember, along with your name?"

"Hi— (cough) Hi, my name is Olivia Wilder."

"Good, good Olivia, do you remember what happened to you?"

"All I remember was that I was driving to the store, then a car hit mine making it roll but after that I do not remember anything."

"Good at least you remember what happened. There is a bit of swelling in your brain, must have hit it when the car was rolling. We are giving you a low dose of medication to get the inflammation to go down. Given your circumstances we cannot provide you with the regular dose."

"Are you saying that my baby is still alive and well?"

"Yes, of course. The baby is still alive and well. I've been monitoring the heart beat and it's great actually. It's too soon to tell the gender of the baby but I would recommend making an appointment soon to get the baby checked by your primary doctor. This way you can find out how far along the baby is and all the other things they do to keep you in check."

"Thank you doctor Dupree."

"Why don't you rest. We tried contacting your emergency contact but there was no response. Should we call anyone else to notify them of the accident?"

"No, it's okay. Thank you."

"Rest Olivia, if there is anything you need, please press the button on the side of your bed and that will call the nurse outside your room."

"Thank you."

I am not surprised that my own mother wouldn't answer as my emergency contact. I could be dying and she is still having fun on her vacation. I really want to call Luciano but I do not want to worry him because I know he will blame himself for not being here with me. My head is starting to hurt so I fall asleep again. When I opened my eyes up, I was lost on where I was but then I remembered I'm in the hospital. I look to my left to find someone grabbing my hand, the person in front of me is sitting down reclining his body into my hand covering his face. I move my fingers to get them out of his hold but as I am doing that, his face comes up to look me in the eyes. Hazel-eyes stares at my blue eyes without a word then he pulls me slowly to hug me. I'm at my breaking point, and tears are streaming down my face. He swipes his fingers to catch any of the tears pouring down, giving me a half smile.

"Baby, I missed you so much. I'm never letting you out of my sight. You don't know how much misery I have been going through since the day you left. This is all my fault, the accident was on me. Please, forgive me Blondie."

"Shh.. Please don't say that. It's not your fault my love. Things happen for a reason. Just take me with you this time, let's do this together. I don't want to be apart from the love of my life. I also have something to tell you."

"Baby, the doctor told me. He didn't mean to blur it out but he didn't know that I didn't know. What didn't you tell me or call me to give me the news?"

" I didn't know about it until yesterday night, well I still wasn't sure. That's why I was going out of the house to the pharmacy today, to go buy some pregnancy test but then the accident happened. When I spoke to the doctor, he confirmed it."

"I can't believe we are going to have a baby! A mini you or me baby. Thank you baby, for making me the happiest in this difficult time. I am going to take care of you and provide for you and this baby."

"Luciano, I love you."

"Olivia, I love you more."

The doctor came in interrupting our conversation, "I see your husband has made you smile." *Husband? Why did doctor Dupree called him my husband? Am I hearing things? Oh no I think my concussion might be getting worse!*

"Doctor Dupree, when can I take my wife out of here?"

Wife? Okay now I'm really confused! What is going on here?

"I want to keep her in observation today until her swelling has gone down completely, then I can sign the papers to discharge her but she will still need to take it easy and rest."

"I want to take her in my private jet to Italy where we have the best doctors to treat her, can I do that?"

"Unfortunately, I do not recommend for her to fly at this moment because of the swelling. It would be best to wait a few days or weeks. I can order some scans to make sure she has fully healed before she gets on a plane."

"Okay, that sounds good. Please do that and thank you for everything."

The doctor leaves the room and Luciano turns back to give me his attention.

"Wife? Husband? What is going on? I am lost!"

"I had to tell them that I'm your husband because they were only allowing family to visit or to even ask any questions about your status."

"Ohh, now I understand. I thought I was going crazy."

"No you're not baby, I just needed to be able to see you and know how you were so I lied to get my way in."

After being apart for a whole two weeks, I wanted to leave this hospital so bad. I wanted to go home with Luciano and I don't mean this home I have in New York, if I could even call it a home because it hasn't felt like home since the day my father got sick and had to spend most days in the hospital. I want to go back home to Italy, that's where I felt more at home with Luciano. Now that I am expecting a baby, Luciano's baby I want to dedicate my time to taking care of my family but I also want to finish my program because I want to feel accomplished. I must have fallen asleep grabbing Luciano's hands as if he was going to leave me again because I had a good grip on him. I slowly shifted my gaze to his beautiful hazel eyes then he kissed my hand.

"Are you hungry? Thirsty? Cravings? I can bring you anything you want."

"My love I think it's too early to get cravings, I actually have been nauseous recently which makes me not want to be near food or any rancid smell. I am a bit thirsty, can I get some water and ice?"

"Yes, I will send Romeo to get us some water and maybe something for me to eat, I haven't eaten anything since yesterday."

I smack his shoulder because he shouldn't be doing that. He should be eating, I know he must have been scared when he heard about my accident.

"How did you hear about my accident, if you were in Italy?"

"I had Romeo come to New York the same day you left Italy. He has been reporting back to me any time you left the house. As soon as he saw the accident, he called me and I got on the jet to be here with you."

"Do you know anything about the person that hit my car? Was it just a civilian or was this one of your enemies?"

"It was the Russians, they had sent me another note, a threat, telling me that they knew you had left Italy and that either way they were going to make me pay."

"What are you going to do? I don't want to stay here alone anymore."

"No baby, you are coming with me. I am not leaving you on your own anymore. I'm going to make some calls to the other families in the organization to see if they can back me up to fight the Russians. Leave it to me baby."

I closed my eyes because I was starting to get tired after all that has happened and the worry of someone endangering my life and the baby's life is exhausting. I have been in this hospital a total of three days now, doctor Dupree has signed the papers discharging me with some medication since the swelling in my head has gone significantly down. Luciano got my things ready, I told him I wanted to go back to my house here in New York to grab a few things. He didn't even complain, he was the most willing to comply with my wishes. When I got to the house I asked Luciano to help me with a suitcase but as soon as I unlocked the door, my mother came out of the living room surprised.

"Liv? What are you doing here? Who is this man?"

"Mom, this is Luciano. Luciano, this is my mother Monique Wilder."

"Nice to meet you Monique, I'm the boyfriend, well soon to be the father of our child."

"Liv? You're pregnant? You really out did yourself in Italy huh? You got a better looking guy, guessing rich and mature and now you are having his baby. Wow! So proud of you! Forget about Christian. When am I getting an invitation to come to Italy?"

"Monique, please stop. You were never a mother to me. You

always treated me indifferently even when dad was alive. Now you want to be a caring mother because you see something that might benefit you! Well I am done. I am moving out of this house, I will talk to dad's lawyer to get the papers ready for me to sign to get what my father left me. You can keep the rest. I'm not coming back. Enjoy your single life, mother."

"Liv, I cannot believe you! Why are you being so mean to your own mother? I want to be able to meet my grandchild. I won't be able to survive with what your father left us. I already spent most of it on you. I don't have a lot, how am I going to survive?"

"Well didn't you just come back from a vacation? Then that means you do have the financial means to take care of yourself. I am not here to support you financially. Whatever you spent on me, I will write you a check once I get my money and for the last time my name is not LIV! You know I never wanted you to call me that but you keep doing it. – Oh yeah before I forget, this house is already paid for, you can get a job if you want to afford paying the rest of the other bills. Goodbye mother."

I packed the few things I needed but Luciano made Romeo hire people to pack up the rest of my other things to take back to Italy. He said I was not coming back to New York so might as well pack everything here to be taken back to Italy. This was the new beginning I desperately searched for and now I am going to get it.

CHAPTER 24

LUCIANO "LUCKY"

I fell onto the seat in the waiting room, the doctor could tell that I didn't know anything about the baby. I am still trying to wrap my head around Olivia carrying my child. I wasn't mad or upset about her having my child because that's what I always wanted, a family of my own. I am upset that Olivia didn't tell me. We could have prevented this accident if she would've told me she was expecting. I could've hired more people to look after her. At this point, what's done is done and all I want is to see her.

"Can I see her now please?"

"Yes of course, when she wakes up she will be happy to see a familiar face but please do not give her any news that could potentially make her heart rate increase. We want her to be calm and restful."

"Okay, thank you."

He showed me the room number she was in. When I went in she was still sleeping. I sat down next to her to grab her hands. I must have dozed off for a couple of minutes, I haven't slept or eaten anything. While I am laying my head on Olivia's hands, she stirred her fingers to get out of my hold. I lift my face to look at her and she is looking at me with those blue piercing eyes. She is emotional, she is shedding tears in silence. I've missed her and she has missed me also. I asked her why she didn't tell me the news but she said she didn't know. She had gone out the day of the accident to get a pregnancy test to confirm it. I told her that the doctor didn't mean to tell me but it just came out because of how I told him that I was the husband. Sounds really nice to be called the husband but that will come eventually soon. We asked the doctor when she will be discharged because I want to take her back to Italy tonight to the best doctors but he told us that he doesn't recommend that at all because of her swelling on her head and also because she is pregnant. He doesn't want complications during the flight. He suggests that she stays to be observed and then once she is discharged to take it easy. Olivia starts talking to me and asking me how I found out about her accident. I told her the truth that I had Romeo spying on her.

"What are you going to do? I don't want to stay here alone anymore."

"No baby, you are coming with me. I am not leaving you on your own anymore. I'm going to make some calls to the other families in the organization to see if they can back me up to fight the Russians. Leave it to me baby."

When Olivia went back to sleep, I went outside the room to call Matteo.

"Matteo, how is everything over there? Are my brothers okay?"

"Yes Lucky everything is okay. There hasn't been any movement from the Russians."

"I'm going to call each family from the organization to help us out in fighting the Russians. Can you call some of your contacts to see if they can help as well?"

"I'm way ahead of you, I did call but I have bad news. They said that since she is not your wife or part of your family that they will not risk it."

"Okay, that's fine. I will call the rest to see what they say. Thanks Matteo."

I started calling the other families but each one told me the same thing as what Matteo's contact had said to him as if they all had the script memorized. There is no way that they do not want to help me just because Olivia is not married to me or isn't my family by blood. This is absurd! The only way of getting help is by marrying her, I didn't want to do this because I wanted to make it special for her but this can't wait. I call all of my contacts again to tell them that as soon as I am back in Italy, I will marry her. They all agree that they will help us get the Russians to back off and if that doesn't work then we fight against them. I go back into the room where Olivia is still sleeping peacefully.

"Baby..? Baby?"

"Yeah.."

"I got in contact with the people in Italy to see if they can back us up to fight the Russians"

"What did they say? Will they help?"

"They will help under one condition."

"What do they want?"

"They want us to get married. Look— I was already planning to ask you and make it special but this is a bit rushed. They will only help if you become my wife or if we are family by blood. What do you say? Do you want to marry me?"

She is speechless at this point, surprised maybe. I want her to know that I want to marry her even if there were no babies, even if the families from the organization weren't forcing us to do this because I love her. I fell for her hard and I don't see myself sharing my life with any other person but her.

"We don't have to baby, I don't want you to feel pressured. We can find another way."

"No— no Luciano! I want to. I want to marry you. Not just because we are being forced to or because you are going to be the father of our child. I want to do it because I love you, you are the love of my life. This much I know and I want to spend the rest of my life with you if that's what you want also."

"Of course I do, baby. You are my soulmate. I've never felt this way for anyone. You have made me see a different world. I want to do this with you hand in hand."

"Then let's do this. As soon as we get to Italy, have everything ready."

"I'll make the call to have everything set. I love you."

"I love you more."

We stayed three days in the hospital waiting for Olivia to get discharged. Once we left the hospital to Olivia's home in Manhattan, we were surprised by her mother's appearance. She discussed some things with Olivia but she did not back down this time and stood up to her mom. When I introduced myself, I already got a weird vibe from her. The things she was telling Olivia were concerning. As soon as Olivia was done with the conversation, she packed a few things but I told Romeo to get people to pack everything so we can take it back to Italy. She will not be coming back unless it's with me. We drove to the private jet and in less than thirteen hours we were back in Italy. I had already sent Matteo a message to get father Torres to marry us in the backyard of our childhood home. Thankfully he agreed because he knew my mother. When we got to the airport, I took Olivia to the penthouse first because she wanted to shower and get ready. What she didn't know was that a beautiful dress was waiting for her in our room. I didn't see the dress because I know it's bad luck. I got showered and dressed in the other room. Once I was fully ready I went to the car to wait for her. The elevator door opened up, I was left speechless the moment I saw her come out of the elevator. She looks beautiful with her dress. I can't believe I am marrying this woman. I got out of the car to open the door for her.

"You look radiant, beautiful and gorgeous. Did you like the dress?"

"How did you know about the dress? I saw it that day when I

went with Abigail to the store. I wanted to try it on so bad but I didn't."

"She was actually the one that told Matteo about it and I told him to buy it in your size because I wanted to surprise you."

"Thank you my love. I love it. Should we get going? I don't want to be late for our own wedding."

"Of course not my lady let's go."

We arrived at my parent's home, the one I have called home since I was a baby. I can't believe I am getting married here. The same place my mother got married to my father. I hold this special place in my heart because they got married in the little altar she had asked my father to make. As soon as we got there, Olivia and I walked hand in hand to the backyard to find father Torres waiting for us. I had my brothers here with me, my father was also here very quietly. My right hand and best friend Matteo is here with Abigail. These are all the people we need. Father Torres asked me if we wanted to officiate the wedding in Italian but I asked him to do it in English so Olivia feels comfortable understanding everything he says. We stand right here hand in hand looking at each other's eyes while father Torres goes through the usual talk about marriage.

"Luciano Salvatore do you take Olivia Wilder to be your lawfully wedded wife, to have and to hold from this day forward, to love, honor, and cherish, in sickness and health, forsaking all others, for as long as you both shall live?"

"I do!"

"Olivia Wilder, do you take Luciano Salvatore to be your lawfully wedded husband, to have and to hold from this day forward, to love, honor, and cherish, in sickness and health, forsaking all others, for as long as you both shall live?"

"Yes! I do!"

Father Torres asks us to exchange the rings I made Matteo buy last minute. We exchanged vows, we wrote while I drove from my penthouse to here.

"By the power vested in me, by the region of Sicily, Italy, I now pronounce you husband and wife. You may kiss the bride."

I kissed my beautiful wife, she was in tears, I am as well because I wished my mother would be here with me sharing this special moment. I wish she could have met my wife, her grandchild and the many more to come. My brothers come up to hug us and congratulate us. Then my father makes his way over but instead of congratulating us he says, "You will regret this son! She is now a weakness that will put yourself in danger. I hope you don't regret this."

"I won't, I will never regret marrying the love of my life. I am glad you are showing me your true self instead of congratulating your son on the biggest day of his life. Thanks dad!"

He leaves after the unnecessary comment. Matteo and Abigail come up to hug us and to tell us that they are so happy for us.

"Lucky, our contacts have responded. I sent them proof of you marrying Olivia and they are more than ready to hit back towards the Russians. We have to do this fast. I know you might want to celebrate but we have no time, maybe after the hit and everything has been dealt with, you guys can go on your honeymoon."

"I agree, I'm sorry baby. This is more important at the moment because this will decide our fate."

"Don't worry husband, I want you to deal with this first so we can peacefully decide our future and the future of our child without exposing them to the enemies."

"I like the sound of that wife. Matteo gets everything ready so we can meet them in an hour. I need to leave Olivia at the penthouse. Have Giani send some of our men to stay with her. Chaos I need you to stay with Olivia as well please."

"Don't worry, I'll go with her."

"Ace, I need you to come with me to meet our contacts so we can deal with this as a family."

"I wouldn't do it any other way brother. I'll be right there next to you."

I left Olivia in the penthouse with my brother Chaos and five of our men taking care of them. I went to meet the contacts with Ace, Matteo and the rest of our men. I am hoping they help us take down the Russians so we can go back to normal and I am able to enjoy my life with my wife. I am thinking of stepping down from the organization and maybe passing it over to Ace since he is still not wanting to settle down. We will see what happens because I know dad is going to be pissed if I tell him about me wanting to step down.

CHAPTER 25

OLIVIA

I can't believe Luciano asked me to marry him at the hospital. After the day I had to get discharged from the hospital then seeing my mom, having that insensitive conversation we had in front of Luciano. I didn't even want to think about it. All that was on my mind during the flight home was about me marrying the love of my life. How did I get here? This seems fast but I don't care. I want everything with him and now more than ever since I am expecting his baby. When we got to Italy, Luciano and I both went back to the penthouse where a beautiful white dress was expecting me. Luciano had mentioned during the flight that as soon as we got back to Italy that we would get married. I wished we could've done it differently but if getting married to him will fix our biggest issue of taking down the Russians then so be it. We are also getting married because we love each other. I wish I could've had my father here to walk me down the aisle. We both got showered and dressed, by the time we got to Luciano's childhood home, we walked to the backyard where we saw not only his brothers but my new best friend Abigail with Matteo by her side. My father in law was also there but his face was not friendly at all. I think he hates me, because he has never been nice to me. Luciano said that Father Torres knew his mother and were really good friends. He will be the one officiating our marriage. Father Torres went over the usual script then with a blink of an eye, we got to the part where he says "You may kiss the bride". Luciano kissed me very passionately, didn't let me go as if he needed all the time in the world to absorb my lips and that kiss was phenomenal. Our friends and family came to congratulate us. Yes, I say family because Luciano's family are now my family too. After Luciano left me in the penthouse with Chaos and five of his men to go deal with the Russians alongside with the contacts of the Italian family organization he works with, I sat in the living room to pray for him and all the people that were going to face off the Russians. I was really scared but I know that Luciano can handle this with all of the people he has by his side.

"Chaos? Can I call you Chaos or do you prefer Alessandro? Do you think Luciano will come home today?"

"You can call me whichever you feel more comfortable calling me. Olivia, let's not think about the worst possible outcome. We know how strong "Lucky" is and how resilient he is when it comes to fixing problems. He will come home! And if he doesn't come home today, he will tomorrow or the day after that. Don't worry, I will stay by your side the whole time he is not here okay?"

"Okay, thank you. I really needed to hear those words. I am really scared of what could happen. I don't want him to get hurt in the process. We are expecting a child together and I need him to be here with me to raise this baby."

"You're PREGNANT!?"

"Yeah, I thought your brother told you?"

"No! That fucker didn't say nothing about you being pregnant. Now I am going to protect you even more because my niece or nephew is cooking there. Do you know what you are having yet?"

"No, it's too early to tell. How about you and Ace get to be the ones to find out the gender and maybe you and your brother can make it a surprise for us?"

"Yes! I love that idea."

A few hours went by, and I took a long nap. When I opened my eyes, Chaos was still on the couch next to me on his phone. I felt relieved to find him next to me because he is like the brother I always wanted and never had. I am an only child. Sometimes I am thankful my mother never had any other kids but I wished my father could've given me another sibling maybe with another person.

"Chaos? Can I ask you a question? I know I might be intruding and it's none of my business but how are you taking the arranged marriage thing your father is forcing you to do?"

"Did Luciano tell you all the details?"

"He told me briefly, I might not know everything but I really feel bad that you have to go through this."

"Well my father only cares about making connections for the family business and since his friend has more connections they made up this whole thing about me marrying his daughter to unify and strengthen our family connections."

"Do you even like or love this girl?"

"No, I don't. I don't even know her that well but I've given up thinking I might have a way out because I don't. Not even Lucky can stop this. I have no say. Unless I rebel against my own father but I could face death."

"Do you like any other girl— I'm sorry I shouldn't ask, it's none of my business."

"No— it's okay, I think I might need to talk about what I've been keeping inside because if I don't, I'm going to go crazy. Are you ready to hear my story?"

"Oh Chaos, pour your heart out. I am here to listen, give you advice if it's needed and most of all, I am not here to judge you so speak freely."

"Olivia, there is a girl I like a lot but it's never going to happen. She is my best friend's little sister. Her name is Elena Rossi, she is Luca's sister. She's off-limits for me. I will never be able to tell her how much I like her, maybe even love her. I have to see her from far away because one, Luca,

*will never accept me for his sister. Two, my father will never accept this relationship because of the arranged marriage. Three, I don't know if she feels the same way about me. I have never really tried anything with her because I am afraid of what might happen. I will get married to someone I don't love and lose Elena in the process because of my cowardliness. I can't stand up to my father or Luca. I don't want to ruin my friendship with him. He has been my best friend since we met in school and he has helped me a lot. But no one dares to go near Elena because Luca has everyone checked and threatened to not even look at his sister in any type of way." (Read more about Chao's story in book 3)**

"Wow, I didn't know about all of this "Chaos", I am so sorry. I can't believe or even think of what you must be going through. If you want any advice, all I can say is that I know Luca is your best friend but I think you should talk to him man to man to tell him how you feel. If he is your real friend, he will support you in every way. Yes, he might get upset but if he really truly wants his sister and your happiness, he will support both of you. Just think about it okay. I am always here if you want to talk again."

"Thank you, Olivia. It was really great to be able to tell you what I was keeping. Not even Luciano knows about this so please don't tell him. I want to be the one to tell him."

"Don't worry, your secret is safe with me."

After my conversation with Chaos, I went to the kitchen to cook something for us because the baby is starving. I made spaghetti which came out delicious even "Chaos" devoured the plate. Once we finished our meal, we headed over to the living room again to wait for any signs of Luciano. I put a movie on to keep my mind busy from thinking the worst. Chaos got a call from Ace which seemed as something went wrong.

"Ace, please tell me how he is?"

I can't hear Ace on the other end but I am starting to worry because we haven't heard anything in hours. Chaos hangs up the phone and looks me in the eye.

"We have to go! We need to go see Lucky."

"What happened? Where do we have to go?"

"He is in the hospital. Ace told me that everything is done. Lucky was able to settle everything with the Russians but got hurt in the process."

"NO! Please tell me he is going to be okay? How bad is he hurt?"

"Let's just go Olivia"

Chaos drove me to the hospital, when we got there I started asking all the nurses to get information on Luciano but no one could tell me anything because they only spoke Italian. I seriously need to learn it if I am planning to live here full time. Chaos grabbed my hand and told me to wait here. That he would do all the talking. He went up to the nurses, spoke to them with so much patience, then in a matter of minutes they were able to tell him which room number Luciano was staying in.

"Let's go Olivia, they said that they have him on the second floor. We will have to wait in the waiting room until he gets out of surgery."

"Surgery?? How bad did he get hurt?"

"All I know from Ace is that he got shot two times. One on his arm and the other on his stomach. Please don't panic. Ace said that it didn't look that bad but he lost a lot of blood."

"How can I not worry! He might die! Please take me to him or the doctor to ask about the surgery. I want to be with Luciano."

We went up to the second floor where we waited for the doctor to come out. Once the doctor came out of the double doors he mentioned Luciano's name but spoke everything in Italian which I couldn't understand. Chaos must have mentioned that I was his wife and that I only speak English because he turned to me to speak in my native language.

"Nice to meet you, Mrs. Salvatore. My name is doctor Pierre. I was the one who took in your husband to do the procedure on him. The surgery went well, we were able to extract the bullet that was in his abdomen. The one on his arm, the bullet went right through, there were no bullets to extract there. He is resting at the moment because he did lose a lot of blood which we had to do blood transfusion for him to stabilize him. I can take you guys into his room now."

"Yes please, thank you."

The doctor took us to the room he was in. When he opened the door, Luciano was wide awake trying to get all the needles and tubes out of his body. Trying to fight it off the nurse.

"Signor Salvatore, la prego di calmarsi, altrimenti non mi lascerà altra scelta che farle un'iniezione per tranquillizzarla."[1] (Mr. Salvatore, please calm down, otherwise you'll leave me no choice but to give you an injection to calm you down.)*

"Va bene! Va bene! Mi calmerò. Quando posso andare?"[2] (All right! All right! I'll calm down. When can I go?)*

"Potresti essere dimesso entro un paio di giorni o entro una settimana, a seconda del tuo processo di guarigione."[3] (You could be discharged within a couple of days or within a week, depending on your recovery process.)*

I walked in between the doctor and him, sat down on the chair next to him and grabbed his hand.

"Please calm down. We don't want your wounds to open back up. Listen to the doctor please."

I don't know what the doctor said to him in Italian but I want to make sure that Luciano is not overworking himself. He needs to rest to get better faster. The doctor nods my way, then he leaves me and Chaos in the room.

"Baby I am so sorry, you have to see me this way. I promise you that it's not that bad. I got hurt before. I feel fine. Please don't worry. You have to think of our baby."

I am crying at this point because I hate seeing him in the hospital. He must have felt the same way when he saw me in the hospital.

---

1. Mr. Salvatore, please calm down, otherwise you'll leave me no choice but to give you an injection to calm you down.
2. All right! All right! I'll calm down. When can I go?
3. You could be discharged within a couple of days or within a week, depending on your recovery process.

I just want him to get well soon. Luciano looks at me crying then he turns to his brother furiously.

"Why did you bring her here? She is pregnant. I don't want her to see me this way or have to worry, she is putting herself and the baby at risk. She needs to rest."

I look at him because he is talking to his brother as if I am not here.

"Luciano! Stop! Don't you dare yell at your brother. He was just following Ace's orders to bring me here. We didn't know if your wounds were bad or not. I would not be able to forgive them, if they didn't bring me here to see you with my own eyes."

Luciano is quiet but I know he understands why his brothers brought me here.

CHAPTER 26

LUCIANO "LUCKY"

Olivia left with Chaos to the penthouse. I felt more at ease sending her home with my brother but I also sent them with five of my guys. As soon as they left, I took my guys, Matteo and Ace with me to meet our contacts. We got to their warehouse, we were met with everyone that was going to help us out with the Russians.

"Thank you everyone for taking the time to meet us here to go over the details of how we will be moving forward with the situation I have with the Russians. Did anyone get in contact with them to see if they could be paid off?"

Then one of the people from the Camorra organization spoke up to say that they tried but they only wanted revenge. I was starting to get upset because they really do want blood to be shed.

"Alright, then we need to have every detail planned out to hit them where it hurts the most, with its people."

We had designed every detail involving everyone's help. When we got done, we all drove our cars to the place we were going to hit. As soon as we got there, the gun shots started. I took cover with Matteo and Ace. I could see all of our people shooting and fighting with their bare hands too. Twenty minutes of us taking cover and shooting. Matteo got up to get closer, I did the same. I could see only a few Russians left, which means that our people have taken most of them down. Then the main leader, the one who sent me those threats came out yelling,

"Lucky! You want blood, revenge and authority? Come to me without a weapon! Let's end this like a man, with our hands."

I don't know why I decided to just go and trust that he wanted to fight with our bare hands. I gave my weapon to Ace, then started to head into his direction but Ace stopped me.

"Are you sure you want to do this? I don't trust them."

"I have to end this! If I don't Olivia and I won't be able to get away from this. If anything happens to me, take care of them okay."

"Them? Who are you talking about? You mean Olivia?"

"Ace, you're going to be an uncle. Olivia is pregnant. That's why I say them."

"Don't worry brother, they will always be taken care of but let's make sure you come back to her or she will kill me instead."

I laugh because it's true, Olivia will kill him for not bringing me back safely to her. I look back to where the main leader is. I slowly start walking until I am half way there. Everything is silent, all I hear are the two gunshots that fly over to me. One hits my arm and the other hits my stomach. I looked down to see where it hit, everything at the moment felt as if it was in slow motion. I looked back up to see him and all I saw was Ace walking in front of me with my gun shooting the main leader multiple times. I don't feel any pain, instead I feel rage but even with my rage I drop down to the floor in seconds. Matteo runs to me putting pressure on my stomach wound. Ace takes his belt off to do a tourniquet on my arm where the other bullet went through. One of the Camorra members comes to me and says, " Lucky we got them, the rest have left or are dead." I nod only because I can't focus with the pain now emerging. My brother and Matteo grab me to pull me up. It feels as if my legs are heavy even to walk but I manage with the help from them. We get into the car, they drive to the nearest hospital. I'm hoping the chief police don't hear about this but I am sure they will since it's a gunshot wound and hospitals are supposed to report it. I will yell at Matteo and Ace if I manage to pull through because they know that they are not supposed to take me to local hospitals. This is the reason why we have doctors on call that we pay to keep their mouth shut. As soon as we get to the hospital everything turns black. I must have passed out from the pain or I am dying from losing blood. I don't remember anything after that, I woke up in an empty room. I start panicking because I have no idea what happened. I have lost maybe an hour or more of my memory because all I remember is the moment when I walked towards the main leader of the Russian organization, after that it was just blurry. Since I am panicking realizing that I am in a hospital which I shouldn't be, I start yanking all of the tubes and needles I have on my body. As I'm pulling them out, the door opens up giving me the best beautiful view.

"My wife" she comes in through the door, then a nurse is on my side telling me to stop pulling the tubes and needles out. I am trying to fight the nurse because all I want is to be able to go back home with my wife. The doctor is speaking to me in Italian telling me to stop. If not he will inject me so I can calm down. I stop because my wife gets in between the doctor to sit next to me. She grabs my hand to tell me to stop, I do! Fuck! My wife is crying and it's my fault that she is here crying her eyes out. I turn to my brother to yell at him for bringing her here. My wife tells me to not blame him because she asked to be here. I'm just pissed she has to see me here vulnerable and not able to defend her or myself if anyone tries anything which I'm sure they won't because my brothers are here and if I had to guess my guys are here as well. It's been a week and a half since I was brought into the hospital. Thankfully my brothers and Matteo paid off the hospital staff and the doctor to keep quiet about the situation. I haven't been able to talk to Matteo or my brothers about what happened after I was brought into the hospital because Olivia has threatened them to not give me any more stress or surprises until I am discharged. I got discharged this morning after all my wounds seemed to be healing perfectly. I am so ready to be home because I want to take a shower, be in my bed and do my wife. I haven't been inside my wife in a long time. I need to feel her, her body, and that ass. Olivia helps me get out of the car, then into the elevator we go. I must smell and look not well kept because it's been long since I showered or cut my hair. When the elevator door opens, I'm greeted by the guys.

"What are you guys doing here?"

"Matteo has five of us making rounds and we switch every five hours. Do you need anything boss?"

"No thank you, I need you guys to go back to work at the warehouse. I'll tell Matteo that I sent you guys back. I don't need anyone in my house at the moment. Thank you guys."

"No problem boss, let us know if you need anything. We are just a phone call away."

"Thanks."

Once my guys leave, Olivia is still next to me wondering what I do next. I tell her to please take me to our room and get clothes ready for me so I can shower and then go to bed. I still feel exhausted even though I told them that I was feeling better in order to be discharged from the hospital. We head into the room where she takes me into our bathroom turning on the water. She decides to leave but then stops mid way to ask if I need her to stay but I tell her to go make herself something to eat since she hasn't eaten anything since we left the hospital. She made herself a sandwich, after I got done showering I went to the kitchen to find she had also done one for me. My stomach was growling at me for not eating this morning. As soon as the sandwich hit my lips, I didn't chew, I devoured it. Olivia keeps eyeing me with those fuck me eyes. I carry my girl to the room to fuck her senseless, I'm being careful not to re-open my wounds while I carry her to the room.

"Strip"

"I missed you Luciano, I don't think I can wait any longer. Please take me."

"What my wife wants, she gets. Now be a sweetheart and open your legs to let me see that pussy."

She is already taking all of her clothes off, I have to be careful with my wound. She is bare in our bed waiting for me. I am about to make her feel so good. It's been way too long. I position myself on the edge of the bed and start crawling up to her body. I take her foot, I start kissing her inner ankle. I take my time kissing from her ankle to her inner thigh. I stop right in the middle of her pussy. I give it a tiny kiss, looking up to see her. She is watching my every move. She has the tiniest bump where our baby is. I caress her tiny bump, then I push her legs apart. I start licking between her folds, working my tongue slowly to get her to the point of climax. She gasps.

"Yes, oh my god baby, yes! Just like that."

"You like that baby"

"Yes! Oh God"

"No God here baby, just plain old Luciano here."

While I'm licking, I push a finger in. She is rocking her hips to the rhythm of my fingers. I push the second one in until she is gasping and moaning so hard. She is about to cum so hard, I stop because I don't want her to cum on my fingers. I want her to be destroyed because of my cock.

"Why did you stop"

"Because I want to be inside you. Open wide baby."

I move up her body. She can't be on top of me because of my wound so I'll be on top. I stroke my dick a couple of times showing her my swollen tip which it's already with pre-cum. She is also super wet which makes it so much easier when I push my dick inside. I can't go hard or fast because of my wound but I will show her how I make love to her slowly. She is gripping my shoulders so hard that her nails are embedded into my skin. I keep thrusting while I am kissing her neck, her lips, her nose and her forehead. I lift myself a little bit to re-adjust myself, I grab her nice pair of tits then I keep thrusting. She's my undoing. I whisper in her ear to get us to that point of explosion.

"I'm almost there baby."

"I am also but I want you to choke me like the very first time we did it."

"What.., I must have forgotten that part?"

"Choke me Luciano! I need to get there one way or another, please choke me!"

I put my big hands around her neck and squeezed. I'm scared to hurt her. What if she passes out on me?

"Don't pass out on me"

"Here, I'm going to show you where to grab me from so you don't cut off my breathing."

She guides my hand where they need to be. Telling me to push one of my fingers on the side of her neck while the other one is also on the other side and then I squeeze a little until she tells me it's enough. I start thrusting faster even though my wound is hurting but as I am thrusting my dick inside her is making me forget all the pain I have.

"Come for me my beautiful girl"

"Oh yeah, yes!"

I can feel her pussy quenching my dick, I know she is to the point of her release. Then she screams my name, making me release my seed inside her causing me to feel my whole body on fire. I am gasping for air, my muscles are tingling and sore but this is the best feeling I have ever experienced . Dropping on to the side of her to rest, we both look at each other after an amazing love making.

"I love you."

"I love you too."

CHAPTER 27

OLIVIA

Once back home after Luciano was discharged, we couldn't keep our hands away from each other. He made love to me, I didn't even know you could feel this way. I never experienced the way he made love to me before. He showed me how to be loved. In the morning, we both woke up at the same time.

"Good morning wifey."

"Good morning my love."

My stomach starts growling and Luciano looks at me as if I deprived myself of food but I haven't, the baby is just hungry every five minutes.

"Get up baby, I'm going to feed you and my son,"

"Hey! Why do you think is a boy? It could be a girl. Also I did eat food yesterday but the baby is just hungry all the time."

"I don't know, I have a feeling it's going to be a boy but if it's a girl, you are going to be doomed because my little princess is going to drain my pockets and my attention."

"Hey that's not fair, I'm your wife!" I tell him in a playful way, even though I would love to see him doomed from the start with his daughter because I know he will be so over protective towards her. I have a feeling that this baby will be a girl. I don't care if it's a boy or a girl because I just want a healthy baby but I am leaning more towards a little girl. Luciano and I get up from our bed to head into the kitchen to make breakfast but we are interrupted by the elevator opening up. Thankfully I am fully dressed because I wouldn't want someone to see me naked plus I know that not many people have access to coming up the elevator unless they are on Luciano's access list. The elevator door opens showing Matteo at the door walking towards us.

"Matteo, what's going on?" Luciano says to him and by the looks of him, he knows that whatever has brought him here is not good news.

"Lucky, we need to talk. In private, preferably."

"I'll be in the room."

I start to walk to the room when Luciano stops me with the answer he decides to give Matteo.

"Matteo, from now on whatever you have to tell me, you can say in front of Olivia. She is my wife and she should be aware of everything going on in the warehouse or anything that has brought you here today."

I stop and turn around to face Matteo, who is nodding at my husband.

"Lucky, we just got word from the chief police that a case has been re-opened because new evidence has come in."

I can see my husband's eyes go wide but I am confused as to which case they are talking about. He starts to sit down, his hands are trembling. I go to stand next to him, I grab his hands for comfort. He looks at me, his hazel eyes look as if they are about to start tearing up.

"It's okay my love, we can face anything together. Please, whatever it is, we can do this together as a family."

"I need a moment, I'll be back."

Luciano gets up to leave, then I am left with Matteo.

"Matteo, care to explain what the hell that was? We are not supposed to upset him until he is fully healed."

"I know Olivia but this couldn't wait any longer. I have been keeping quiet since he was in the hospital. I haven't said a word to anyone about this because I didn't know how Lucky wanted to handle this. I don't know if he wants to be the one to tell his brothers or anyone for that matter."

"What did the chief police tell you?"

"Well, he— he said that.."

"Come on, you heard my husband. He told you that I should be aware of any news or anything you want to tell him."

"I know Olivia, It's— it's just hard to say them out loud. Lucky has suffered from this for a very long time. I don't want to see him lose his mind because of it but he deserves the truth."

I'm starting to get scared myself because it seems pretty serious for what Matteo is about to tell me and my husband. I don't want Luciano to lose his head but if it's needed then we will face this as husband and wife.

"Are you going to tell me? Or are you waiting for Luciano to get back?"

"I think Lucky already might know what this is about. Well the chief police came to the warehouse while Lucky was in the hospital. They wanted to talk to him but I told them he was out of town for business, if they could relay the message to me since I am his right hand. They told me to have Lucky come by the station, to give them all the details which weren't given to me but they did say that they had new evidence that came in about his mother's death."

I am speechless because Luciano told me the story about his mother's death, when we were first living here together. One of those nights where I couldn't sleep, we talked for hours, then he poured his heart out telling me the way his mother's death happened. I am sure that at this very moment my husband is raging on the inside because if there is new evidence, I am hoping they tell him who is responsible. Matteo leaves to go back to the warehouse because Luciano has not come back after all. Once Matteo left, I went to try to find him because he wasn't in any of the places he usually likes to be in. Not the gym, not his office, not my art studio and not our room. Where could he be? I decide to leave him be, he will come to me when he is ready. I go into our bedroom because I still have a few things to unpack. I barely was able to get the things Luciano had people packed from my house in New York. While I am putting things away, I hear the bedroom door open. I silently turn my gaze to see him standing there with bloodshot eyes. I get up as quickly as possible to reach him. I hug him tightly, I know that's what he needs right now.

"Baby I am here for you, don't worry okay."

"Did Matteo tell you anything after I left? I haven't gotten the courage to call him to find out."

I tell him what Matteo told me, I can see the way his mood changes. I know he needs to find out and I know he will leave now to do that so I don't stop him because this is important to him.

"Will you be back tonight?"

"I don't know but you won't be alone, I'll have my guys stay while I am out."

"Can you call me when you get there so I know you are safe?"

"Yes, I will. I love you. Don't wait for me, okay."

Then he is on his way. I try to distract myself by going back to unpacking but after an hour I was done with everything. I'm in the living room trying to keep myself busy so I don't start thinking bad things. I go to grab my phone off the counter. I go into my contacts to look for Abigail's number, then message her.

"Hi Abigail, what are you doing?"

"Hi Olivia, everything okay?"

"Yeah, Why wouldn't it be?"

"Because you never text me, you always either call me or show up at Matteo's house."

"Sorry, I have been a bad friend. With everything that has been going on, I feel I haven't had time for anything. Do you want to come and join me?"

"You by yourself? Where's Lucky?"

"He had to go into the warehouse to talk to Matteo. I feel very lonely. I don't want to sound clingy but I miss him. I only feel safe with him."

"I'll be right there okay, don't worry. I'll have one of Matteo's guys drive me there."

Thirty minutes later, Abigail was being sent up the elevator to my floor. As soon as she came into view, I couldn't hold it together. I started sobbing so much, I blamed the pregnancy hormones. They are making me a weak bitch! Abigail just held me and told me to cry until I couldn't anymore. I think I cried more than when I was kidnapped.

"What's going on, why are you crying Olivia?"

"Matteo came to talk to Luciano about his mom because I guess a police officer told him they re-opened the case. I am so sad for Luciano because I know how much it hurts him to talk or remember his mother. I think it also has to do with me being pregnant. Surprise!"

"Oh, he came to tell him already? And what the hell, Olivia why didn't you tell me? A baby!! OMG!"

"You knew? Did Matteo tell you? Of course he did huh, but yes I am pregnant with Luciano's baby"

I look at her with a smirk, which she is trying super hard not to engage with but I know that she and Matteo have bonded and I am pretty sure he likes her and so does she.

"Bitch! Before we even talk about this, you have to tell me! What's going on with Matteo??"

"Nothing, we are just really good friends."

"Really good friends.. Like really good fucking friends with benefits or just friends?"

"Just friends, nothing has happened between us. I know that I live in his house but he has always been respectful and has never insinuated anything."

"But you want to though? Right?"

"If I am being honest, yes! I want him to make a move but he hasn't. I don't think he likes me like that."

"Abigail, you are beautiful. Of course he likes you like that! Maybe he is just giving you your space to figure it out and maybe he wants you to take that first step."

"I'm always so awkward around him when we are alone. I don't know what to do. I get nervous, stutter and make myself a fool."

"Are you still dealing with your nightmares and going to your therapist?"

"The nightmares have gone away but I am still going to my therapist to deal with letting any men touch me. I flinch anytime Matteo's men do something unexpectedly around the house but I am trying my best to minimize being scared but I do want Matteo with me every step of the way. He has shown me patience, kindness and he is the only one that makes me feel safe and secure. Just like how Luciano made you feel basically."

"Then show him how much you appreciate Abigail. Matteo has every girl after him, I noticed when we went to the nightclub that he doesn't pay attention to them but they do to him. If you don't want to lose him, I suggest you take that step so he knows how you feel."

"I will! I need to stop being scared. I don't want to lose him. I told him that I feel as if I am taking advantage of him for staying at his house for free. He told me that I can stay until I get better but I don't want to get better if that means that I have to leave his house."

"Then tell him Abigail, I am sure he feels the same way about you. You can see it in his eyes every time he looks at you. You can hear it, every time he talks about you. Go be happy Abigail. I want to see you happy."

"Thank you Olivia, I think I'm going to text him to come home so I can talk to him."

"Yeyy! Tell me all about it tomorrow okay. Go! Go!"

Abigail gets up to leave. I had already forgotten about our conversation, which made me distract myself from the issues we have.

CHAPTER 28

LUCIANO "LUCKY"

We have an amazing night of making love, showing her all the love by taking care of her every way possible. I am head over heels for my wife. She's making me crazy. I eagerly anticipate the moment we meet our baby and discover if she resembles her mother or me. After a delightful night, we awoke to the sound of her stomach grumbling. We both got up to make something for breakfast but we were a bit startled when we saw Matteo get off the elevator. I knew there was something wrong as soon as our gaze connected. He rarely comes to my penthouse, he always waits for me to go to the warehouse to tell me about anything. If I have to guess since I haven't been to the warehouse, he could not hold the information any longer. Matteo starts talking, telling us that the chief police have decided to re-open a case because new evidence has been released. I already know what case they are talking about because it's the only one that has gone through them. It was impossible for our family to cover anything because all the neighbors, cameras and anyone that was there saw the whole thing, where those people dropped my mother's dead body in front of our mansion. I wonder what new information has come out because it's been years. I look at Olivia then at Matteo. My wife comes to stand next to me to grab my hands but at this moment I just want to be alone. I decide to leave because there is no way I can deal with my feelings in front of them. I head to the hidden stairwell that goes to the roof. I only come here to think or when I'm really stressed out. Hours have gone by, Olivia must be looking for me. When I get back into the room, she is unpacking all of her things in our room. She stops whatever she is doing to let me know we can face anything together. I tell her that I have to go to the warehouse to talk to Matteo. I tell her that I am leaving my guys in place to take care of her. She nods in silence knowing that I need to do this. She tells me to go because she knows I need to figure this shit out. As I am pulling in front of the warehouse, I see Matteo outside telling our guys where to take the next shipment.

"Hey we need to talk, come to the office when you're done here."

"I'm done here, they know what to do. Let's walk together."

Inside the office I take a seat gesturing to Matteo to do the same. We are both looking at each other in silence, no words are coming out from him or me because he knows that as soon as he starts I will turn weak but I need to be strong.

"So.. Tell me what did the chief police tell you exactly."

"He didn't tell me much, he wants you to go to the station to debrief you on the new evidence. The only thing he said was that they have re-opened your mom's case because new evidence came in."

"Okay, I'm going to go to his office now. Can you call to see if he is in?"

"Yeah, give me a minute to figure it out."

He makes the call letting me know that the chief police officer is in fact in his office. I tell Matteo that I will be on my way and from there I will go home, and for him to take care of everything here. I get in my car dreading every step. I park my car in one of the available spaces then head inside. A nice lady takes my information asking me if I have an appointment but I tell her that I was requested to come by. She tells me to have a seat. Fifteen minutes later Chief Police came into view, telling me to follow him into his office. I take a seat, he introduces himself as Stefanno Bianchi Chief Police.

"Thank you for coming, I went by your warehouse but they told me that you were out of town."

"Yes, sorry we didn't get to talk then. Can you tell me what new evidence has come out."

"Oh, straight to the point I see! Well I can tell you that someone was apprehended recently due to a different charge and in order to get his sentence reduced he started spilling all of his secrets. He verified that he was sent to kill your mom and to also drop her off in front of your house. He actually gave us the name of the person who ordered the hit but we still are working on evidence before we make an arrest."

I could not believe that I was this close to knowing the truth. I swore to make anyone pay for the death of my mother and now I will get to know who did it. I hope he tells me but I have a feeling he won't.

"Who was responsible for my mother's death?"

"Oh Mr. Salvatore, you know I can't tell you that yet! I already provided you with enough information at the moment with what we are doing. I will make sure that once the evidence can prove that the person mentioned is responsible then you will be the first to know because I will need to make the arrest myself."

"Thank you. Please keep in touch."

"Mr. Salvatore, I don't have to tell you to keep your hands out of this correct! We are always looking into your businesses and anything that has to do with you so keep a low profile if you don't want to get into trouble."

"Don't you worry, you won't be hearing from my businesses. Everything I do is legal. By the way, how did you learn English this good?"

"My wife is from the United States, California to be exact. I lived there for a few years then I had my daughter there but I didn't really like the "American life". I brought them back to Italy to have a better future. Why do you ask?"

"Because when I got here, you didn't speak to me in Italian. You went straight to English."

"I guess I didn't realize I did that. I usually speak Italian here at the station but with my daughter I speak English and maybe it just felt more natural speaking the same language since your right hand man mentioned you all speak English."

"Well Thank you again for the information. I'll be expecting a call from you chief!"

With that I got up from my seat ready to go home to my wife. By the time I got home, Olivia was nowhere to be seen. I went to the room but she wasn't there. I looked at her location and her phone was saying she was still in the house. I went up to her studio room, finding her in a tiny sheer outfit. She isn't wearing any bra or underwear, only that sheer dress. As I enter the room she lifts her hand to stop me from walking any further. I am already hard as a rock. My lady wants to play, I can play.

"Hi baby, I missed you. I thought we could play a little to distract you from all our issues."

"Damn baby, I like the sound of that. Come here!"

"No, I want to play a little game. Do you know how to play "I spy"? If you don't, I can teach you."

I nod because I used to play this game when I was little with my brother Ace.

"Will there be a punishment if I don't answer right?"

"Yes, every time you get it wrong you will lose an item of clothing. If I lose you can pick the punishment for me."

"I like this game! It's a win-win for us. Let's start."

"I spy with my little eye something red."

"Your dress string?"

"No, wrong. Please take off one item of your clothes off."

I take my socks off because I know that will piss her off. While I am taking it off, I am smirking at her. I never leave my gaze because I want to see her reaction.

"Hey, that's not fair! Okay, continue it's your turn."

"I spy with my little eye something blue."

"Mm.. Is it my portfolio?"

"Yes it is. Your turn." I'm making it easy for her because I want to be naked before I can actually give her a punishment.

"I spy with my little eye something green."

"The paint?"

"No! Luciano you're not even trying. It's not the paint. It's my nails."

I went on to take another item of my clothes which I chose as my shirt. We kept going until I was fully naked. She guessed every single one except for the last question. Now I have to punish her but all I want is to take her to bed.

"Your punishment is going to be to suck me off and then after you're done I will make love to you the only way I know how."

She gets on her knees looking at me with her long lashes. Grabbing my thighs to pull herself to be right in front of my cock. She starts stroking it which causes me to groan. I need this release because I am too stressed with everything. She sees that I already have some pre-cum on the tip of my dick, she takes her finger to smear it all over her lips. That just gets me harder. She looks me in the eye while she is kneeling down and asks if I am ready. I simply nod because I can't put anything into words. She strokes my dick once then twice, goes to put it in her mouth and she moans making my dick vibrate.

"Damn baby! You are taking me so well."

"Mhm..." moans again.

"Just like that baby. Can you put it a little bit further?"

She goes to do what she's told and I can see tears from her blue eyes, then she makes a gagging noise which makes it even hotter but I know my length so I try to retrieve back but she grabs my thighs to keep me in the same position. I feel like I am going to cum inside her mouth but I don't want to. I pull her up to stand in front of me.

"I don't want to come in your mouth, I want to come inside you."

"Take me to the room then."

I pick her up putting her legs on my waist while I'm carrying her to our room. She is kissing my neck and playing with my hair.

"I love you Luciano."

"I love you too Olivia, you are my everything and this baby is our love combined."

As I lay her in our bed, I get on top of her centering myself in between her legs. I play with her pussy with my fingers doing circular motion just how she likes it.

"Please Fuck me!"

"Greedy girl but because you said it so nicely, I will fuck every inch of you."

I push my cock inside her, making her gasp each time because she has to adjust to my size. I move in and out of her making her and myself feel good. I take it out, then slam it back inside because my girl likes it rough but I also don't want to hurt her or the baby. Shit the baby! Can I hurt the baby?

"Babe, can I hurt the baby if I do it too hard?"

"I don't know Luciano, I'm going to be a first time mom so I don't know the do's and don's but I'll make sure to call for an appointment to ask all of these questions. Now, shut up and keep fucking me!"

"I like this side of you! So bossy!"

CHAPTER 29

LUCIANO "LUCKY"

I woke up super early to make breakfast for my wife. She is still asleep since we didn't get much of it since we were horny all night. I made something simple for her, I made myself some coffee. While drinking it I started to reminisce about all the times we had breakfast with our mother. Tomorrow is my birthday, another day spent without her. Maybe now I can actually enjoy it with the love of my life and soon my child. I will make sure this baby has all the love and everything I was not given as a child. I want to make sure I keep my mother's traditions and show my son or daughter that as the father I will always be there no matter what. I will never tell them that crying is a sign of weakness like my father said to me once. I will always protect, provide for them. I get out of my thoughts when I see Olivia with my shirt which fits her as a dress. I don't even know if she is wearing anything under that but it leaves it to your imagination.

"Morning Blondie."

"Hey, you haven't called me that in a while. I like it but I also prefer wifey."

"Okay, then good morning wifey."

"I was able to get an appointment today with the doctor to check on the baby. Do you want to come or do you have somewhere to be today?"

"Of course I'll come, I want to be there for you every step of the way. Let me get ready."

"I will get ready too. I'm going to shower. Do you want to shower with me?"

"Thought you would never ask!"

We both shower, got ready and twenty minutes later, we are inside the car going to our appointment. When we got to the place, we waited for a few minutes then we were taken inside of a room with a bunch of screens, the lights were dimmed. Olivia laid in the patient's bed, then the doctor came in. She introduced herself. I had to do all the translations because the doctor only spoke Italian. Olivia looked nervous, I grabbed her hands to intertwine them with mine. Telling her that everything is going to be okay. The doctor put a jelly looking liquid on her belly then started to do the ultrasound. She let us know that the baby is healthy and everything looked good. She told us that we needed to wait until around four months to know the gender of the baby. The doctor sent us home with supplements for Olivia to take and told us to come back in a few weeks. I drove back home but on our way home my phone started ringing so I answered it, the call came through the car's speaker.

"Lucky? Where are you?"

"Matteo, I am driving home with Olivia. You're on the car's speaker. What's going on?"

"You need to come to the warehouse now!"

"What happened?"

"I can't tell you over the phone, just get here as soon as possible."

I took a u-turn back to the warehouse with Olivia. Matteo's voice sounded frantic, I am not risking Olivia by leaving her home and me not being able to protect her. As soon as I got to the warehouse, red and blue flashing lights just outside it.

"Fuck!" I punch the steering wheel because at this point I am thinking the worse. Maybe they caught up into our illegal business or something else bad happened. I tell Olivia to stay in the car, I get out as Matteo is getting out of the warehouse with the chief police.

"What's going on?" I say to Matteo and the chief police

"Mr. Salvatore, do you have a minute to talk to me?"

Fuck, I was thinking it was going to be about the warehouse but I think it's about my mother. I look back to the car where Olivia is. I tell Matteo to stay with her while I take the chief police officer to my office to talk.

"Sure, follow me. Please call me Luciano."

"Luciano, I came as promised. We were able to find the evidence and the proof that points everything to the person responsible. It's going to come as a shock because we never expected this but I want you to know that I am heading as soon as we are done talking to make the arrest."

"So... who was the bastard that killed my mother?"

"I am so sorry to tell you this but it all points to your *FATHER*!"

"My FATHER? What the fuck! He couldn't have! There is no way!"

"I am very sorry to be the one to tell you but your father wired money to the person we arrested and he provided proof of the transfer and the messages between them. There is also a call from him demanding they scare your mother a little and that he will be sending the money to their account."

"No! No! N—!!" I go numb, I can't feel my legs. This is not possible. How can my father have done this? He loved her right? Why did he do this to her, to us. We were just kids. My brothers and I lost our mom so young. This is not possible."

"Can I see the evidence please. I won't believe it until I see it and hear it."

"I thought you might say this. Off the record, I never showed you this okay. I know how hard it must be to hear that your own father is responsible for the death of your mom. This is the reason why I brought the evidence with me. I will show you but you cannot tell anyone I did this."

"Sure, show them to me!"

He takes out his phone to show me the picture of the wire transfer, then the messages he must have taken from the actual phone. Then he slides to the next picture which is the recording of the phone call that was recorded. When it starts the voice is not recognizable but as the person keeps talking I realize it's my father's voice! My own father! I lift my hand to stop him from keep listening to the recording. He puts his phone away then silently looks at me with pity. I'm in my head right now. I don't want him to get out of my office because if he does, he will go straight to arrest my father. Going to jail or prison it's too easy of a punishment for him. I want revenge even if he's my father. I go to sit down behind my desk, pull my phone underneath the table to message Matteo.

"Go to my father's house right now. Have my men take him to the warehouse's basement. No questions asked! Do as I say!"

"Got it boss, I'll leave Olivia with Giani. I'll be the one to do the job. Be right back."

"So what is your procedure now? What does this mean for my father?

"Well, I will go make the arrest now, he will stay in jail unless he pays for bond but we will have a court date set for him to get prosecuted. Your father will most likely go to prison for the rest of his life. I just ask that you stay here, to not intervene in the arrest."

"Okay, thank you for everything. Could you please call this number once you have made the arrest. I want to be the one he looks at in the face when he gets put in jail."

"He will most likely have one phone call, I am guessing he will try to call you or any of your brothers or maybe his lawyer."

"He sure will!"

Stefanno Bianchi leaves my office leaving me sitting down completely numbed. How could my father have my mother killed? How are my brothers going to feel about this? I get my phone out again to shoot a message to them.

"I need you both at the warehouse in my office in thirty. NO EXCUSES!"

Ace: "I'll be there in fifteen."

Chaos: "I'll be there in fifteen minutes as well."

There's a knock on the door, letting me know one of my brothers is behind this door. I tell Olivia to open the door. After I sent that message I went outside to look for my wife to bring her into the office because she is part of this family as much as my brothers are. Olivia opens the door finding both of my brothers there. I tell them to come in and have a seat.

"What's going on Lucky? You are scaring us. You never message us to come to the warehouse unless something is going on. Are you sick?" Ace says without taking his gaze from me.

"No, I am not sick. I have brought you here because there is something important I need to tell you guys. This cannot wait."

"Okay, just spill it!" Chaos demands.

"Chief Police was just here a few minutes ago to tell me that our mother's case has been re-opened because new evidence has come in."

"What the fu—!"

"Let me finish, don't interrupt me!"

"Go on.."

"He got proof of the evidence from someone that was just recently arrested, he kind of negotiated his way to lessen his sentence by telling the chief police that someone sent him to kill our mother. He provided a wire transfer, messages between the person who sent him, and a phone call recording of the person telling him what to do with our mother. The person responsible for the death of our mother... (I sigh) It's— It's our father."

They both are speechless just like I was. I know the feeling. I turn to look at my wife and she has put her hands in her mouth, she is also speechless but I can see tears in her eyes. Chaos is facing me, his face is red. They are both about to be raging because we are talking about our own father killing our mother.

"Where is the old man now? I want to have a talk with him!" Ace says.

"The Chief police is on his was to make the arrest—"

"No! He is not getting away with murder by just going to jail! He needs to suffer, just like he made us suffer!" Chaos yells.

"Don't worry! The chief police is not going to find him. I had Matteo take him out of the house before they could do the arrest. They must be on their way! He will be in the basement but we have to think about this really hard and plan out what we want to do to him. He is still our father, even if we want to make him pay, we will need to make sure it's none of us shedding blood in there because of him. If we do something with our own hands, there is no going back."

"I don't know about you but I want to make him suffer, for all the things he has done to us, to me especially but also to our mother!" Chaos exclaimed.

"No, we will do this my way! No one is fucking touching him until we talk to him and he confesses what he did!"

About thirty minutes have passed. Matteo called me as soon as he got to the warehouse with our father. I sent Olivia home because she kept yawning. She must have been really tired, she is pregnant and pregnancy can make you sleep all the time. Once our father was in the basement, my brothers and I started walking together to meet the devil himself. As we were going to the hidden stairs to go down to the basement I got a call from an unknown number. I pick up the call, Chief police are on the other end.

"Luciano? Your father was not in his house. He must know we are on to him, he probably has fled but I will keep working to get him arrested. Please let me know if he gets in contact with you."

"I will! Thank you sir." Knowing that I will never call him to inform him about my father, we will deal with this our way.

CHAPTER 30

LUCIANO "LUCKY"

My brothers and I continue to go down the hidden stairs to the basement. We all stop at the first door where we see Matteo stand outside.

"Lucky, your father is very concerned about us bringing him here. We did not restrain him or anything because all we did was take him out of the house, we did however blindfold him because no one knows about the basements since you did them once you took over. He thinks he was taken for his own protection to a hotel."

"Don't worry, Thanks for everything. We will handle this from here. Matteo can you have everyone take the rest of the day off, go home and rest for today. Have everyone come back tomorrow, ready to work again."

Matteo takes off leaving us by ourselves. We take a deep breath before opening the door. The door swings open finding our father seated down on the chair drinking his coffee.

"My sons, what is going on? Why was I taken out of the house so abruptly? I couldn't even finish the food I was eating nor pack some clothes."

"Dad don't worry, we took you out from there because there are threats and we need you to be safe."

"Then why is this door locked? Am I a prisoner? What is it that you are not telling me?"

"Chaos, go bring dad another cup of coffee, we need to talk about what's going on." Chaos goes to make the coffee which he already knows that we are putting on a small dosage of sleeping medication.

I take the seat right in front of me, I stare at him without words coming out of my mouth. Ace is in the corner, fisting his hands as he cannot contain himself. Chaos comes back with the coffee then gives it to dad. He starts to smell it as if he is checking for any signs of us tempering with his drink. He is not stupid! But why would he doubt us his children? I go to speak to tell him he will need that drink for the amount of time we will be here talking but instead he starts drinking. Great! Shall we! Let the revenge begin!

"Dad, can you tell us from the beginning how mom got caught up in the middle of this situation where she got herself killed?

"What is this about? Why are you asking about your mother? We have gone through this before! All I know is that she left the house after an argument we had, then hours later I received a message saying someone had her but I didn't think it was true so I didn't pay for the rescue. An hour later your mother's body was dropped off outside the house, where the police showed up and had me questioned but then said I was able to go. Why are we remembering this awful memory of my wife? I don't want to remember that, she was my everything and I miss her every single day."

"LIAR!!! YOU ARE A PIECE OF SHIT!" Ace yells with tears in his face.

"Ace, we cannot lose control. Let me deal with this." As much as I want to do what Ace is thinking, I can't. I have to think smart.

"Just tell us the truth! We have evidence that you were the one who sent people to kill her! WHY! WHY OUR MOTHER??" Desperately begging for him to tell us.

He keeps drinking his coffee, unfazed because that's our father!

He has never had any remorse for anything that he does. Not when he hired older women to take advantage of me and have me lose my virginity, not when he made me kill the very first person to show me that I was a man now, not when he used to treat us so badly, not when he used to physically hit my brothers, no remorse ever. I slap the coffee out of his hand, smashing it against the wall, causing for him not get any side effects of the sleeping medication we put in it.

"You have only one option! To tell us the truth. If not, face the consequences!"

"Boy! I am your father! You can't do anything to me!"

"Do you want to bet? Don't try me because I am losing my patience."

"Fine! I will tell you! Your mother and I were having an argument that day because someone had messaged me a picture of her with another man talking. I confronted her about it and she said that he was just a friend. I didn't believe her. I was also upset at her for the way she always raised you guys, to being noble, kind and weak! I got really mad when she tried to tell me to stop doing illegal business because she will report me to the police. That was my tipping point. I didn't plan to kill her, I just wanted to scare her a little. But the person that I sent to do it, he said that she fought for her life and took off his mask. She wasn't supposed to see his face. The guy gave me no options, he said that he had to do what was best for him. I offered him money which I did wired but then he had her lifeless body dropped off in front of the house. I kept quiet because you guys were little and if they would've taken me then you would've been on your own maybe taken by the police to put you into new families, maybe separate you from your brothers. I didn't know what else to do. I couldn't explain this to a sixteen year old nor an eleven year old or a three year old. I did what I thought was best."

My brothers and I are speechless. I cannot believe our father just confessed all of this to us. I have nothing to say to him. He killed our mother, even if he was just trying to scare her. He should've never let it get to that point. Hearing my father say she fought for her life makes me so mad to even see my father in the eye. I get up from the table opening the door because I need to get out of here! Ace and Chaos both go out with me.

"I don't know what to do with him. I don't want us to shed any blood because we are not like our father. I think it's best to let him go back home, I will call the chief police to have him arrested and they can deal with him."

"As much as I want him to hurt and take all of my anger on him, I think you are right Lucky!" Ace says

"I agree with you guys, I don't want to take matters into my own hands because we weren't raised like that. Our mother would be rotting if she knew what went through our mind about what we wanted to do to him." Chaos says.

We go back in, my father is looking at each of his kids like it's the last time because It will be for me. I don't ever want to see him.

"We are going to take you back to the mansion, I will call the chief police to have you arrested. You will do nothing! You will wait there until they have successfully taken you into custody. You will spend the rest of your miserable life in prison to pay for the death of our mother! You got that!"

"Yes! I will do as you say. I know I have to pay. I have one thing to ask, please?"

"Go ahead, make it quick."

"Can you give me fifteen minutes so I can just sulk about everything that is about to happen to me. I promise I won't do anything, I just want to walk through our house one last time, reminisce every corner I spent with your mother and then you can have them arrest me."

"Whatever you say old man! Fifteen minutes only!"

We took him to the house, we were all inside the car waiting for the fifteen minute timer to end but I went ahead and called the chief police to tell him that our father is back home and to be here soon. The only problem is that as soon as the timer hits ten minutes, leaving five minutes left on the clock. The whole house exploded, it bursted into flames. Every single space of the house exploded as if he had bombs in each room of the house, I am not sure how that was possible or maybe he just lit things on fire making them explode. We could feel the waves of the explosion just outside the gate. Both of my brothers looked at me. We got out of the car and started running to the double doors. We opened them but the flames were everywhere, everything is scorching hot. There is a lot of fumes making it hard to see. We try to go in but then all of a sudden our father runs out of the house, his whole body is on fire. I take off my jacket, I start hitting his body with it to get the flames to stop but it's impossible. It seems as if he poured something on himself to make it easier for him to burn.

"Ace, Lucky! My things! The house is burning. I am the only one still living here and my things are still inside!"

"Fuck, let me call the fire department. Try to get the hose from the backyard to pour whatever we can."

The chief police gets there while all of this is happening. He is yelling "what happened", I try to explain to him very briefly while he is calling back at the station to get more people out here. The fire department and the rest of the police get here in no time. They start pouring water everywhere which made the fires subside but there is still fumes everywhere making it hard to see. They have told us to wait by the gate, we are not allowed to be in there since they have to assess the situation whether it was intentional or planned. It has become a crime scene at the moment. We are not allowed to go near it and I feel bad for Chaos.

"Alessandro, look at me! You can stay with me until everything gets settled okay." I am grabbing him by his face so his focus turns to me. I never call him Alessandro because he always said to call him Chaos as if he wanted to be reminded of what our father called him.

"You never call me Alessandro, maybe I should let people call me that since our father is not here anymore to keep reminding me how much Chaos I have always caused. Hey— does this mean that I no longer need to go through the arranged marriage our father did with his friend?"

"I don't know, I'll get in contact with his friend to explain the situation. I will let him know that the deal is done since our father doesn't make decisions anymore."

The chief police comes outside to the gate where we are waiting.

"Your father has passed away. They did all they could but the wounds from the fire were too much on him. He died in agonizing pain. I am sorry for your loss. I will have everything go through our station, please contact the station to get more information on what needs to be done after this. The fire department has put all the fires out from the house but it's destroyed. The house is off limits for a couple of weeks until our team has analyzed everything. I will call you once that's done. If you have any questions, you know where to call me. Ahh— Ace! Stay away from my daughter!"

I look at Ace, he has gone pale with that comment. What is going on with him and his daughter? I look at both of my brothers then we are hugging next because I think that is all we need at the moment. We didn't even cry or feel bad at the notice of our father passing away. He deserved it. Now all I want to do is go home with my brothers and see my wife, live a normal life. Maybe it's time to leave the business behind just as our mother begged our father. At this very moment I cannot think of a better way to honor her by letting go of all this illegal shit for the sake of my family, my brothers, my wife and kids. I just know that we will need to take it day by day because I am sure that Ace will not want to leave his nightclub. I am pretty much set for the rest of my life. I have made more money than I could have hoped for. There's no need for me to keep this as a family business. I look at my brothers,

"Let's get out of here! Let's have a family dinner after this shit show, I just need my brothers with me."

"Let's go! I am so down!" Ace says

"Let's go! I love you guys!" Chaos says.

"We love you too!"

EPILOGUE

LUCIANO "LUCKY"

2 YEARS LATER

I can't believe that everything we went through two years ago was something I'll never forget. From finding out who was responsible for the death of my mother, to having my first child, to stepping away from the family business, to Olivia getting her degree in fashion design. I never expected my brothers to be okay with me stepping away from the family business. Ace didn't want to be involved in the imports and exports of the drug business. He told me he would gladly be okay just being the owner of the nightclub. He closed the brothel which we used mostly for money laundering. Ace wants to settle down and form a family. I can't wait until he has his own kids because he loves coming to our house to spend time with my kid and he teaches her bad words in English and Italian. And yes! I had a baby girl, blonde hair, blue eyes just like her mama. We named our daughter Luna Salvatore, she is the most precious little girl that has stolen my heart. I love having brothers because they are very protective over her.

"Luna come here sweetie, let's go walk max, I think he needs to release some energy."

"Yeah, Daddy"

Max is our german shepherd, we rescued him from the shelter. He was going to be euthanized. Thankfully we got there on time and we took him. He is the best dog I could've possibly gotten. He is our protector but mostly Luna's, he loves her.

"Hey, wait for me. I am in need of a walk myself. This baby is punching all of my organs all damn day but mostly at night. I am trying to see if I can get him to wake up with our walk."

"Of course baby, you are always welcome to walk by our side. Always remember." Showing my wedding ring to her because even though we got married to save her life, we still said our vows and we meant them. We just recently found out that our second baby is going to be a boy. Olivia wanted to name him since I named Luna. She wanted a traditional Italian name, so she went over multiple baby names and decided to name him Niccolo Salvatore. Olivia stopped working after she found out she was pregnant with our second. She is still doing pieces on the side to sell on her website and made to order depending on what people want but she is fully invested in being a stay at home mom for now. She is a great wife, sister in law and mother. I couldn't have picked better, she is my soulmate. After Olivia gave birth to Luna, we decided to move out of the penthouse because it was no place for a child. We bought a big house near the beach in the outskirts of Palermo. We moved to Mondello beach which is about twenty minutes from Palermo. I still get to see my brothers since we are still close by. I do not need to worry about money since we have a lot saved up from years and years of working for the family business but I still help Ace with anything he needs around the nightclub but I mostly stay home with my family. I enjoy being with them every single day. I made a little niche in the backyard to remember my mother which came in super helpful when showing and teaching Luna about her grandmother. She goes there every time we go out to play in the backyard and kisses the picture we have of my mother. Talking about grandmothers, Olivia's mom called her a few times apologizing for being a horrible mother but she was still asking her for money because she did not want to work. Olivia felt bad once and sent her money but now she thinks she will send it any time she asks for it. She has not met our daughter and we are planning on keeping it that way.

"Oh no Luciano!"

"Baby you peed yourself, you could've told me you needed to pee. There's a bathroom not too far from here."

"No honey, I didn't pee myself. My water just broke! The baby is coming!"

"Oh shit!!! Let me call my brothers so they can stay with Luna."

"Oh shit!!" Luna says.

"No baby, you can't say that word. Daddy didn't mean it. That's a mean word okay." Mouthing sorry to Olivia because she is already about to cut my dick off because my brothers keep teaching her bad words and now I'm saying them in front of her. I call my brothers but they don't answer. I go to call the other one and the phone is picked up by the last ring.

"Hey I need you to come to my house ASAP! Olivia is in labor and I need you to stay with Luna and Max."

"Oh shit, I can't at the moment. I'm dealing with some fucking shit at the nightclub. Have you called Chaos to see if he can go there first?"

"Yes you fucking idiot, I called both of you dumbasses but you are the only one that answered. I need you please. Just have someone deal with it in the meantime until Chaos can be here then you can go back to dealing with your shit."

"Okay dumbass! I'll be right there in twenty. You owe me big time because the bullshit I'm dealing with right now needs to be solved by today. Call the other dumbass and tell him to go to your house."

I hang up and look at Olivia, she has a death stare. I'm about to tell her what's wrong but then I'm interrupted by Luna.

"Daddy, fucking idot" She laughs as she says the word

Now I'm screwed. I am getting murdered by my wife. I keep

cursing in front of Luna and she keeps repeating it. I pull her up and I whisper to her to stop saying bad words that daddy is saying because those are bad. She looked at me with puppy eyes and then started crying. Oh no! I can't take it. My daughter's cries are my weakness. She is fucking adorable. Then I hear Olivia clearing her throat to get my attention.

"Ahem!"

"Yes honey."

"I am in pain, hello?"

Twenty minutes later my brother gets here to take care of Luna and Max. I get in the car with Olivia to the nearest hospital. Not even three pushes later then we hear the cries of our son Niccolo. I just can't believe I am living in a world where I get to do life with my beautiful wife Olivia, my two kids and my brothers. I am beyond grateful to have them in my life. I can't wait to see what our future holds together. I wouldn't mind having another child. I always wanted to have three kids since we are three brothers, I wanted my kids to have siblings as I did. I never really did tell you guys why my nickname is "Lucky". My brothers named me that when they were young because they used to say I was their lucky charm.

"What can I say! I'm the luckiest big brother."

THE END

Did you enjoy Lucky Trigger?
Please leave a review

BONUS

Are you ready for Joey "Ace" Salvatore? Check out the next book in V. Elias's The Salvatore Brothers Series, Ace's Underworld! Coming Soon...

Coming Soon... A story for Matteo and Abigail. Keep up with all the news and updates about my upcoming books by going to my website and subscribing to the newsletter. Can't wait to give you a little snippet of their story in Book 3 of The Salvatore Brothers Series.

ABOUT THE AUTHOR

V. Elias is a romance book author. She is a writer and a reader. Her favorite subjects in school were English/Literature and Psychology. She has a degree in Social & Behavioral science and a minor Criminal justice. Has a background in Psychology. She began writing in journals, then on her notes app but never thought she would write to publish. V. Elias is an introvert and so many of the reasons she never took a chance on publishing because she did not have the courage to do so, there were so many insecurities until one day she began doing videos of book reviews on social media. One of her books review videos now has more than 176.3k views. This year she decided to take a leap of faith to do what she loves and risk it all. Live your dream readers! She decided to pour her heart and soul into her writing to share her passion for romance books, to share with the world that you can do anything you set yourself up to.

You can connect with V. Elias on:

- https://veliasauthor.wixsite.com/veliasauthor
- https://www.instagram.com/v.eliasauthor
- https://www.tiktok.com/@v.eliasauthor

Leave a review on Amazon or Goodreads:

- Amazon reviews
- Goodreads reviews

ALSO BY V. ELIAS

Lucky Trigger is V. Elias first book of the series, The Salvatore Brothers Series book two and three will be live on kindle unlimited soon. The Series are all stand-alone mafia romance but is best enjoyed if it's read in order.

- Lucky Trigger is book one, Luciano "Lucky" and Olivia
- Ace's Underworld is book two, Joey "Ace" and Aurora "Rory" (Coming Soon)
- The Scars of Chaos is book three, Alessandro "Chaos" and Elena (Coming Soon)

V. Elias debut novel, a short story known as a novella. Romance, Blind date, Infertility, and love at first sight. Released date April 15th, 2026 on kindle unlimited and paperback. Spanish Edition released April 15th, 2026.

- So this is love!, Lucia and Julian
- Esto es amor!, Lucia y Julian

www.ingramcontent.com/pod-product-compliance
Lightning Source LLC
LaVergne TN
LVHW050540160826
845677LV00011B/2108